SOS Docs

Bound by tragedy… Saved by love!

Chase Barrington and Ethan Reid share a tragic past. Now working tirelessly to save as many lives as they can, these heroic docs are thrown together on their latest humanitarian mission. But this time, they won't only be helping others…

As Chase and Ethan meet and fall for two very different women, could this trip be their chance to find their own opportunity to heal?

One passionate night changes lone-wolf Ethan's life forever in

Saved by Their One-Night Baby
by Louisa George

Can one passionate kiss convince Chase to leave the past behind in

Redeeming Her Brooding Surgeon
by Sue MacKay

Both available now!

Dear Reader,

I was absolutely thrilled to be asked to write another duet with Louisa George. This is our third duet and it was as much fun as the previous two, because we get on so well and can brainstorm our stories and characters without banging heads.

The backstory we came up with for our heroes is heartbreaking and had us in tears just thinking about it, so I'm hoping it has the same effect on our readers. Have the tissues ready just in case.

When Kristina and Chase first meet on board the ship that provides medical care for refugees, Chase is too busy working through his past to have much time for this beautiful doctor who's come on board for twelve weeks. But three months is a long time to be squashed in a small space with someone who sets the blood racing through your veins and your heart out of kilter every time you see her.

Kristina pushes Chase's boundaries, and he can't resist her. To the point he takes her home to meet his family when he's never taken anyone there before.

I hope you enjoy these two and their story as they both put the past behind them and move forward— together.

I always love hearing from my readers. Drop by at suemackay.co.nz or suemackayauthor@gmail.com.

All the best,

Sue MacKay

REDEEMING HER BROODING SURGEON

SUE MACKAY

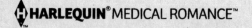

Recycling programs
for this product may
not exist in your area.

ISBN-13: 978-1-335-64166-3

Redeeming Her Brooding Surgeon

First North American Publication 2019

Copyright © 2019 by Sue MacKay

Printed in U.S.A.

This book is dedicated to all those amazing people who give their time and skills to helping those less fortunate. You rock.

**Praise for
Sue MacKay**

"Ms. MacKay has penned a delightful novel in this book where there were moments where I smiled and moments where I wanted to cry."
— *Harlequin Junkie* on
Resisting Her Army Doc Rival

PROLOGUE

SCREECH. THUNK. METAL hitting concrete.

Men shouting.

'Accident!'

'Quelqu'un est blessé!'

'Aidez-moi!'

Bang!

A swinging metal chain swiped the crane it was attached to, swinging outward.

More shouts and yells.

'Cherchez le médecin!'

Kristina Morton spun around and began running towards the noise, her heavy pack bouncing on her back, aggravating damaged muscles.

'I'm a doctor,' she shouted to the security guard standing at the steel gate accessing the wharf where a freight ship was being loaded. Tapping her chest, she said, 'Doctor. Me.'

The man shook his head. *'Non.'* He pointed to another ship. *'Docteur.'*

'Oui.' Pointing in the same direction, Kristina

uttered one of about five French words she knew. 'Yes, I'm a doctor joining that ship. *Doctor*.'

Rolling her shoulders back, she slid out of the straps of her pack and dug into a side pocket, handed over her wharf pass. Written in French, it did say she was a doctor. Didn't it? She hadn't taken a lot of notice when she'd received it along with other documents at the hotel reception desk where she'd stayed in central Marseilles last night.

The lock clanged open and the gate swung wide, allowing a man in fluorescent overalls to run frantically towards the *SOS Poseidon*, the *Medicine For All* charity ship Kristina had been bound for.

The guard called after him with urgency and Kristina took the opportunity to slip into the sealed-off area, her pack knocking against her good leg. It wasn't hard to see what'd happened. Seventy metres along the wharf pieces of a metal cage were spread across a wide area, and from under what looked like a side of the crate protruded a pair of legs, while the man's helmet-encased head was under the edge bar. Men were clustering around, waving their hands and yelling at each other.

'Oh, hell.' She ran faster, reached the men and dropped to her knees with a hard thump. Ignoring the pain that set off in her injured thigh, she shouted, 'I'm a doctor.' 'Doctor' sounded similar to the French version; surely they'd get the message? Too bad if they didn't, she was already observing the man crushed under the steel strops meant to hold the side of the cage together, except they'd sprung apart on impact. 'What's his name?' she asked without thinking, and got a surprise when someone replied.

'Antoine. Is he unconscious?'

'I'm not sure.' Reaching under the metal for his wrist proved impossible, it was too far in, so she pressed a finger on his carotid. 'Antoine, can you hear me?' Damn. He wouldn't understand her. 'Can you talk to him, see if he's responsive?' she asked the man who spoke English, before focusing on the pulse rate. Normal. So far so good, but still a long way to go.

She couldn't understand what he said to Antoine but she recognised the flickering eyelids. The helmet had done its job. A quick appraisal showed blood seeping through Antoine's trousers from his groin where a metal shaft had lodged. Her heart stuttered as the memory of a similar injury swamped her. Automatically her hand went to her thigh and rubbed down the ridge of scar tissue.

'I told him you're a doctor. I'll get some men to lift this.' The man now squatting next to her knocked the cage.

'Get them ready, but don't move it yet. Antoine's bleeding. Removing the pressure could cause a haemorrhage.' Bleeding out wasn't an option on her watch. Not again. The guilt at not being able to prevent Corporal Higgs dying had not dissipated so much that this didn't unnerve her. Not that she'd been in any position to help the soldier, being disabled herself, but doctors were meant to save people, no matter what. 'I need something to make a wad to press over the bleeding.'

Moments later Kristina was handed a small bundle of shirt pieces folded into squares, while another man was tearing his shirt into strips to tie the wads in place. She wouldn't think about the hygiene aspect, containing the bleeding was the priority.

'Thank you. *Merci.*' The odd angle of Antoine's left leg indicated a fracture above the knee. 'Be careful, don't hit this when you take the grill away.' She pointed to the rod.

'It's attached. It'll pull out.'

She hadn't noticed that. Now she'd prefer the man unconscious. He needed morphine, fast. 'Can you send someone to the *Poseidon* and get a doctor to bring drugs for pain and some oxygen?'

The man looked along the wharf. 'Someone's coming. He's got a bag and a small tank. Is that what you want?'

'I hope so.'

The man was there in an instant, barely puffing despite his sprint. 'I'm a doctor.' He hunkered down on the opposite side of Antoine's legs.

'Me, too,' Kristina told him. 'I was headed for the *Poseidon* when this happened. Kristina Morton.' She held her hand out.

His hand gripped hers briefly, firm *and* electric.

Shock ripped through Kristina. Rubbing her arm, she stared at him. What just happened? He'd sent fire through her veins with a handshake? Unreal. She was supposed to be focused on a man in distress, not this one with the most intriguing face she'd ever encountered.

A startled look was reflected in the dark depths of his eyes, too. Had he felt that spark? 'Chase Barrington, SARCO.'

Shock of another kind rocked her. This was Chase? The man who caused his family heartache on a regular basis? No one had told her he was hot! 'I met your sister when I was a locum at Merrywood Medical Centre. I finished a fortnight ago.' His brother-in-law, Jarrod, was one of the partners there.

'Libby told me.' He gave her a sharp look. 'Bring me up to speed.' Chase was taking charge.

Typical. She'd worked with enough male doctors in masculine environments to know the signs. 'There's a rod intruding into Antoine's groin that's attached to the grill. I'm hoping you've got morphine in your pack.'

'Yes, and compression pads.' Chase nudged the kit with his foot, and focused on the man needing his attention.

Leaving Kristina to get her breath back and stop feeling flustered by Doc Barrington's touch. She could tell him to get the pads himself, but time was of the essence, not her pride. Finding the morphine, she read the date out loud, gave the vial to her counterpart to cross-reference before drawing up a dose. Once administered, she opened packs of compression pads, ready for the grill to be lifted away.

Chase was methodically checking for further injuries on Antoine's body without jarring the grill. No wasted movements, his lean body muscular without being heavy. Picture perfect. So not good for her pulse. Deep breath, concentrate— on Antoine, not the SARCO. But he was so distracting. She closed her eyes, opened them and watched.

Without stopping those long fingers moving over Antoine, he told her, 'Ribs staved in, fractured femur and arm, blood loss from where the humerus protrudes, and I don't like the look of his mouth. It's possible he's bitten his tongue.'

He was good, and thorough. Impressive in more ways than that magnificent body.

She nodded. 'Let's do this. The sooner we can get to him the better.' It was hard not to glance at Chase for another take on those muscles shaping his loose T-shirt but she managed. Looking behind to the men waiting to help, she said, 'On the count of three lift the grill—very slowly.'

The moment their patient was free she was pressing a pad onto the wound in his groin. 'The femoral artery's torn. Is there a catheter in your kit I can put in to keep the blood flow in the artery?'

'Unfortunately not.' Chase was gently removing the man's helmet in preparation for putting a facemask on Antoine for the oxygen. 'I haven't got a neck brace either.'

Kristina continued working on the haemorrhaging, making do with what was on hand, but the sooner help arrived in the form of a well-equipped ambulance the better. 'Has anyone called the emergency services?'

'*Oui,*' replied a man hovering in the background.

Like magic, the sound of a siren filled the air.

Kristina didn't relax. Antoine wasn't out of trouble by a long way.

A quick glance showed Chase working as hard, diagnosing all the injuries while keeping an eye on the man's breathing. There was a determined look on his face that said, I am not letting you die, Antoine. Something they had in common.

But anything else? She doubted it. The little she'd heard from Libby and Jarrod indicated she and Chase were like north and south. She was looking for a place to settle down and feel as though she belonged, a place where she wouldn't be thrown aside at anyone's behest, while this man apparently did not have the time or inclination for stopping still. He was driven. Not that she'd been told by what.

The ambulance squealed to a halt beside them. Instantly paramedics were moving in, asking questions in rapid French she didn't understand. Continuing monitoring their man, she left Chase to answer them.

'How's that bleeding?' he asked her moments later. 'Still bad?'

'Yes.' She nodded around the relief that getting Antoine to hospital fast was now happening, as long as the paramedics didn't take too long preparing him for the trip there.

'We've done all we can. The paramedics are taking charge,' Chase said, his hands clenched on his thighs, his jaw tight, and his eyes fixed on the two men as they put a cardboard splint on the broken leg and a brace around their patient's neck. He wanted to remain in control, was itching to continue working on Antoine.

Kristina knew that feeling but moved back, knowing she would not be thanked for doing anything else. The paramedics knew what they were doing, and were used to working without the luxury of all the equipment an emergency department came with, but couldn't they get a hurry along? Glancing at Chase again, the same thought was reflected in his steady green gaze.

When Antoine was finally loaded into the ambulance, relief loosened the tension gripping Kristina and she was free to walk away, if only her feet would move. Staring across the now quiet wharf, her gaze fell on the ship she'd be working on for the next three months, sharing the space with a man who had her hormones in a lather already. She'd be toast by the end of her time on board.

It had been Jarrod who'd suggested she do a spell with *Medicine For All*, instead of taking on the locum job in the far north of Scotland she'd been half-heartedly considering.

Watching men and women walking up the gangway laden with heavy packs for the start of the next three-week stint, tiredness enveloped her. She was weary of constantly moving from place to place, locum position to locum position, and not having somewhere of her own to return to after each contract finished. MFA was merely another diversion. It was harder this time because she'd finally found what she'd been looking for.

The quaint town of Merrywood and its friendly folk had sucked her in, made her welcome and comfortable in a way she hadn't known since she was ten and her family had imploded, leaving her bewildered and alone. She'd wanted to stay on, continue working at the medical centre and buy a cottage on the riverbank, only there was no job once the doctor she'd been covering for returned. However, Jarrod had told her to stay in touch and drop in when her time with MFA was up as he might know of a position for her. She planned on doing exactly that, fingers crossed and expectations high.

'Time to go aboard and meet everyone.' Chase stood beside her, legs tense, his eyes constantly on the move.

'I'm looking forward to this.' The organisation did amazing work with refugees and other people in need of medical attention in horrific parts of the world, and to be a part of it was awesome. And in case Jarrod didn't come up with the goods, she'd have time to research small towns and medical centres in the south of England in the hope of finding that same enticing family-orientated atmosphere she'd found in Merrywood.

Why did she look to the man beside her? He

wasn't the answer to her need to settle down. From what she'd heard, Chase Barrington could no more stop in one place than he could knit a blanket for a baby.

'What made you decide to give *Medicine For All* a go?' Chase asked as they walked out of the secure area.

'I'm getting tired of locum work. I start to feel settled and then have to pack up and leave again. Jarrod suggested MFA and how I might fit in. Once I started delving into the organisation I knew I had to give it a go and contacted Liam.' The director had been effusive when she'd volunteered. Though again she'd be moving on afterwards.

Fit in. Chase studied the slender woman before him. Get under his skin, more like. His brother-in-law had been chuckling when he'd told Chase how Kristina Morton was perfect for the summer operation in the Mediterranean. Yes, he'd known who'd put her up to signing up and until now had had no problem with it. All doctors were welcome any time. But now Chase had to question what fates had put *this* doctor on *this* mission. 'You want to get away from GP work?'

Her laughter was soft and sweet, and stirred him. Not that he wanted to be stirred by a beautiful woman. Or any woman. He'd put her where he put any female who managed to tweak his interest—out of his mind.

'Not at all.' Her shrug was tight. 'It's just that I would like something permanent, somewhere to get to know people beyond their headaches and high blood pressures.'

Good. The complete opposite from him. 'You like ships? Being at sea, getting tossed around in storms?'

Another shrug. 'Wouldn't have a clue, but I'm about to find out.'

There was more to this. For someone who wanted permanence she seemed to move around as much as he did. Not that he was about to ask her about it. That spoke of being interested and getting involved. Not his thing. 'Liam's a great advocate for our organisation. Without him we wouldn't get half the volunteers that sign up.' If not for Liam, who knew where *he'd* be working right now? For all he knew, it could've been in Africa, Asia, New Guinea, anywhere there were lives that needed to be saved. That was his mission in life. Not that he'd ever make up for the loss of his best friend, Nick, but he would keep trying. One day the guilt might run out. Might.

'I didn't stand a chance once he started in on me,' the woman matching his strides admitted. Then her eyes went a bit sad.

He wasn't asking about that either. They'd

reached the security gate. 'Yours?' He nodded at a pack and roll mat the guard held out.

'Thanks.' She stretched for them.

'I'll take those.' Chase reached out at the same time. His fingers skimmed across hers before wrapping around a shoulder strap on the pack. A jolt of heat caught at him. Spinning sideways, he swung the pack over one shoulder and hooked the mat under his arm then headed for the ship, ignoring Kristina and the inferno in his blood. That was the second time he'd felt the heat around her.

Unfortunately she kept up with him. 'I don't expect you to carry my gear.'

Chase stopped as quickly as he'd taken off. 'I'm not trying to show you up as incapable. I'm exercising the manners I was taught as a lad.' If not in the polite way his father expected.

'It's just…' She hesitated, seemed to be thinking how to say whatever was bothering her. 'I'm ex-army. No one ever carries your pack there.'

He'd read in her CV about Kristina being ex-military. And the evidence was in front of him in her upright, controlled deportment—and apparently in her determination to carry her own pack. Because she'd heated his blood and stirred him with her soft laugh, he was going to rock her boat. 'You're not in the army now. I'll carry these to the ship.'

'Fine.' Her mouth drifted up into a lazy smile,

stirring him tighter. He should've walked right past the blasted gear and its owner. It was as though she was poking him with sharp pins to wake him up from a long, deep sleep. But he wasn't asleep and as far as he could tell Kristina hadn't come armed with anything sharp, except maybe her tongue.

Chase pulled on his co-ordinator's hat; only way to go. 'I saw in your CV that you've worked in quite a few different medical jobs.'

The smile slipped away slowly, painfully. The light that had begun shining in her eyes faded. 'I have.'

Again, there was more to this than the simplicity the words suggested. If she wasn't saying anything else it had to be that something had happened to affect her badly. He'd respect that, because he understood too well about keeping fears close, and pain closer. Suddenly he wanted her smile to return. 'On board we tend to treat one another kindly, no ordering anyone to do anything.'

Her nod was abrupt. 'Good.'

Try again. 'The refugees are going to love that calm manner you showed with Antoine.'

'That's me. Calm throughout a crisis, a bit rocky afterwards.'

'No one would know that from helping Antoine.' There. A subtle lifting of those lips he'd have missed if he hadn't been watching for it. His heart lightened. Then her perfume wafted across his nose and he pictured pine cones on the fire at home. Pine and roses. Yes, the strange mix that was home was this woman's scent. A scent he was not going to get out of his senses in a hurry. They'd just met, and she'd found a way to get under his skin already.

It didn't bode well for his sanity when they'd be crammed together for weeks with all the other medical staff in the small spaces that were the ship's medical facilities. They'd probably end up hating the sight of each other. It happened. There was little privacy, no space to think without being interrupted. Having no alone time did a number on everyone, especially on those used to their own company; like himself. Something about how Kristina held herself, self-contained, suggested she'd fit into that group.

Chase began striding towards the ship again. 'I think most people have arrived.' He automatically scanned the people at the gangway. And tripped. Ethan Reid stood at the bottom of the gangway, looking directly at him.

Chase's heart began a low thump, thump. So much of who he'd become was tied up in that man. And Nick.

The past charged at him in waves, winding him, curdling his stomach, raising the fear of not being able to save those he loved, bringing ice and snow pushing away the warm summer air, suffocating him. Death. Not his. Nick's. The crippling guilt.

I can't do this.

Yes, he could. He had no choice. He'd been the one to put out the feelers, asking Ethan to step up to the promise he'd made way back then. *If ever you need me, call.*

Right now Chase rued that phone call, even though it had been about helping others. But it was done. He needed to start moving forward, towards Ethan, the man he had saved instead of Nick, and the hideous past they needed to dispel, or at least subdue so they could work together. Would they be able to talk about what had happened that fateful day in the Alps? About why certain people had survived when others hadn't? Why Nick had died, and Ethan had survived? Why he'd had to make that choice about who to save even when there really was no choice? Turning his back on Nick as the last breaths left his body had haunted him ever since, and made him go over it again and again looking for a way to change the outcome.

'Chase? Are you all right?' Kristina's question seemed to come from miles away. Her hand gripped his arm, shaking him, soft and endearing in her touch.

'Yes,' he lied, stunned at how easily she saw past his barriers, how she was there with him. No one did that. No one. He shrugged free of her hand, his eyes firmly locked on Reid. *Don't think you're getting the chance either.* His past rose higher, flared, threatening to overwhelm him. Bile soured his tongue. 'I've got to talk to that man.' It was that or charge past him to shut himself away in his cabin and not come out for six weeks. *Six weeks.* Why had he made that blasted phone call?

Ethan was walking towards him like they did this every day, but as he got closer Chase saw the tight lines around his mouth, the rigidity in his shoulders. Chase's heart was still drumming that slow, heavy rhythm as he nudged his feet forward. 'I'd have known you anywhere.' Even after sixteen years.

'Same.' Ethan did the unexpected. He embraced Chase, tight, strong, hard.

Tears sprang to Chase's eyes. He refused to let them out. Refused. And won, by a scratch. Stepping back, he stared at the other man who'd haunted him for so long. Thump, thump, in his chest. This was relief over finally meeting up. It was time. Not that he had any expectations of this being an easy ride. No, the coming weeks were going to test patience and forgiveness on both their parts.

'I'll take my gear,' came the voice of female reason from behind him.

He barely noticed Kristina lifting the weight from his shoulder, although as she began walking away and he was watching Ethan, she slipped into his mind, sitting on the edge, like she was not going to be easy to ignore. Right now that was about the only thing he was certain of.

Hell, Nick, what have I done?

CHAPTER ONE

Six weeks later

'KRIS, GOT A MINUTE? I'd like you to look at my patient.'

Kristina Morton ignored the man, even when his voice was like fingers picking at keys on a piano. Only that morning everyone had returned on board from a three-day break, and she'd missed him way too much for someone she wasn't involved with.

'Kris, over here,' Chase called again, a little less friendly and a lot louder.

She continued walking through the over-crowded cabin towards the steps leading out on deck. About once a week he used the abridged version of her name, winding her up something awful. He hadn't a clue to the depth of anger and hurt being called Kris caused her—neither was he about to.

'Kristina, your attention now.'

Kristina's back straightened, her chin jutted

forward and her arm began lifting in a salute. *Stop. You're not in the army now.* Being the person in charge of personnel on this ship didn't give Chase the right to shout at her. Or shorten her name. But, she sighed, he had finally used the name she answered to. Slowly turning, she asked calmly, 'Which patient do you want me to see?'

Determination radiated out of eyes that reminded her of an English forest on a damp day. Chase wasn't used to being ignored. Everyone complied with his requests no questions asked, but then they weren't usually delivered as abruptly. So it was *her* that got his boxers in a twist. Good. Because he certainly kept her panties in a knot. Those sparks she'd experienced on day one of this adventure hadn't died down one bit. Instead, they'd got brighter, sharper, hotter during the weeks of working together. Neither of them had made a move to explore where that raw attraction might lead. She did her best not to be alone with Chase, and suspected he did the same, but the relentless ache was getting to her, and she spoke more abruptly than she'd intended. 'Is it the pregnant lady needing help?'

'Sorry I yelled,' he growled around a wary smile. 'You didn't seem to be hearing me.'

'Really?' She tipped her head sideways, locked her gaze with his and tried to deny the surge of longing those eyes brought on. Another six weeks of working alongside him. Keep this up and she'd either dislike him intensely or have gone raving mad with desire by the time she left the ship for good. Somehow she doubted dislike would make it onto the ladder.

Chase blinked and his face relaxed some more. 'Yes, that lady. She won't let me near. No doubt because I'm male.'

'You know that's not uncommon.' The pregnant women who arrived on the ship via the rescue efforts weren't used to men pressing their bellies and listening to their unborn babies through stethoscopes.

'I keep hoping for a different outcome.' Chase smiled ruefully. She knew he ached for these people like she did. 'This woman doesn't speak English.'

'I'll find Zala and ask her to explain what we're doing and if it's all right to continue.'

Chase's chin lifted a notch. 'Zala?'

Kristina smiled to herself. Chase wasn't the only one who got onside with the refugees effortlessly. He just thought he was. 'She arrived yesterday. I overheard her asking for water in English.' Not that it had been easy to understand her mangled pronunciation, but when she'd handed the girl a bottle of water she'd received the most beautiful smile imaginable and a garbled thank you. 'I don't know how much she understands but any is better than none.'

'Agreed. Bring her in and see if we get any further with our patient.'

Kristina gasped. Why hadn't her senses warned her Chase had moved closer? Suddenly her body was getting up to speed with the fact that this man was too near, sharing the same air as her. Damn the attraction for those arms and legs, for the flat stomach and strong jawline nailing her feet to the floor. She'd spent six long weeks trying to kill off the annoying magnetism Chase's body had for her. Her mind had it worked out—he was not a man to get close to. He was self-contained in every aspect, appeared to work every hour day and night, was on a life mission to save people no matter where that took him—or so the gossip went. Gossip that fitted with what Libby had told her. She couldn't risk falling for someone who couldn't settle down in a place for more than one Christmas in a row. Because, while she wasn't any better, she was at least working on it.

Time to try some other tactic for moving past the unusual longing to get to know this man who dominated her mind so much. He was all wrong for her, as she was for him. He didn't have time for anyone who wasn't a patient in need of his extraordinary medical skills, so she had to stop thinking about him in any role other than the director from whom she took orders. *Instructions, not orders.* Whichever.

Dreaming about his body and what she'd like to do with it didn't change the fact she had no room for people who didn't have time for her. There'd been enough already, starting with her parents. Adding someone else to the list was a recipe for disaster, especially when she had an uneasy feeling that she could get a weeny bit too intrigued by Chase.

Out on deck Kristina made her way through the hordes of people waiting patiently in the shade provided by tarpaulins strung from bulkheads to railings to be seen by the medical staff. Her heart ached for them and made her grateful she could help with their untreated deep-tissue injuries, burns from fuel, malnourishment, infections. Thank goodness Claire had left the ship. Her pregnancy made her vulnerable to illnesses she wasn't prepared for. Now, there was someone whose life had changed since coming on board the ship. Claire had found love and a wonderful future to look forward to with Ethan.

Kristina shoved aside her envy and focused on reality. 'Zala,' she called.

'Hello?' The girl glanced at her from under lowered eyebrows.

'How are you?' She spoke slowly in order to be understood.

'All right.'

'Good. You had food?'

'Yes.'

Kristina again looked around at the people sprawled on the hard deck, hunger, fear, worry in every pair of eyes watching her. If only she could fix everything for all of them. Back to Zala. 'Can you help me talk to a woman who needs a doctor to examine…? To look at her baby.'

'I…' Zala tapped her chest. 'I say what you say my way?'

'Yes.' Kristina nodded. 'I'll keep it simple.'

'I don't know what you mean.'

'That's all right.' She reached for the girl's hand, hesitated. Touching didn't always mean the same thing to people from the Sudan as it did to Westerners. Retracting her hand, she said, 'Come with me.'

Back in the treatment room, persistent Chase had returned to his pregnant patient, holding out a water bottle and talking softly, even though not a word was being understood. Around here it was all about the tone of voice and not the words. 'I think we're in labour,' he told Kristina.

'How do you know?'

'The way her body stiffens every three minutes.'

Yea, she got her first smile of the morning. He should do that more often, it lightened the green of his eyes to that of a summer's day in the fields. And set her heart dancing. Damn.

'She's not going to want you here.' Kristina focused on the woman, avoiding getting tangled up in Chase's searching looks and that blood-warming smile. 'Do we know of any problems that could make delivery difficult?'

The woman caught her breath and pushed around the tightening in her extended belly.

'Minor fever. Exhaustion that's probably due to the pregnancy.'

'Fingers crossed the baby hasn't been infected with anything.' Kristina indicated to Zala to move closer. 'This woman's having a baby.'

Zala nodded as if to say, So what? Seeing a birth was probably part of everyday life for her. There'd be no racing off to a hospital or calling out the midwife where she came from.

'I'm clearing all male staff to the other side of the room,' Chase said. 'Call me if you need anything.'

'I don't think I've got much of a role here either,' she said, before turning to the woman Zala said was called Marjali. Light stretch marks on the skin covering the extended abdomen confirmed this was not her first pregnancy. 'She'll know what to do as much as I do.' *More than I do.*

Sweat shone on the woman's forehead as she pushed and groaned. Zala sat at her other side and chattered in short, sharp sentences before telling Kristina, 'Four babies. Two alive. On boat with her and father.'

'Are they all right?' What had happened to the other children? Kristina's heart squeezed. She'd never get used to the despair these people faced daily. There were times she felt so inadequate she wondered if it would be better to leave them to what they were used to and not offer promises through medicine. But she hadn't become a doctor only to turn her back on anyone needing her skills.

When her twelve weeks with *Medicine For All* were up she'd head back to England. She wouldn't do another stint on the ship. It was too distressing. Many of the medical people who worked in the organisation coped well with—or managed to hide—their emotions. She struggled to do either.

A sharp cry brought Kristina back to the marvel that lay before her. The baby's head was crowning while Zala chattered, excitement filling her dark eyes.

Kristina smiled as she watched the baby inching its way into the world. What was it like to give birth? To have a baby of your own? To hold him or her in your arms for the first time? She never gave much thought to it, afraid she wasn't capable of being a good mother. Her own mother had taken her to Los Angeles when she'd left her father, but had been quick to hand her back when the new man in her life said he'd marry her as long as *Kris* wasn't part of the package.

The man's wealth spoke strongly to her mother's lifelong fear of ever being poor again, and Kristina had been returned to England and her other parent, who'd immediately deposited her in boarding school because he'd been too busy to be there for her.

A sharp cry from Marjali and a tiny new life with the cutest face and a smattering of tight curls was delivered with one final push.

'Oh, he's beautiful.' Kristina's eyes moistened as she cut the cord and took the baby to check his temperature and general appearance before placing him on the scales attached to the nearby wall. Back home, with a weight of two kilograms, he'd have been admitted to the neonatal unit. Here all they could do was get nutrients into him so he might put on a gram or two before leaving. It could've been worse given the circumstances. Laying baby across his mother's tummy, she said, 'You made it look easy.'

Zala looked perplexed. 'Women have babies. It's normal.'

'You're right.' Again she wondered about the odds of having her own baby. Strange how she was thinking about this. She hadn't found a man to love her no matter what, let alone have a baby with, a man who wouldn't leave her to fend for herself while he went off to follow his own dreams. That should be enough to knock her attraction to Chase out of the paddock. Since joining this ship she'd seen him playing with some of the youngsters who came on board, laughing with them, chasing a football and making sure each kid had a turn at scoring a goal. He understood them, enjoyed them, so why not want a family?

Crossing to a cupboard for cloths to clean Marjali, she passed Chase. 'All done. One new little man has arrived in the world.'

'That was fast. Does the baby appear healthy? In as much as you can tell without doing tests?'

'A bit underweight.'

'We'll keep an eye on him while he's with us.' That was Chase-speak for making sure there were extra rations for Marjali over the coming days. What happened after she left the ship was out of their hands. Their job was to deal with these people for the time they were in their care, and then move on to the next intake.

'Life's so complex, yet Marjali makes this seem simple,' she sighed, watching the woman cradling her son. Zala sat cross-legged, still talking non-stop, reaching out to touch the tiny bundle pushing into his mother's breast, not knowing what to do when he found a nipple. But his mother did. Soon he was suckling. Whether he was getting anything nutritious was unlikely given Marjali's malnourished condition.

'Very unlucky for some,' Chase said. Then looked directly at her, stealing her breath. 'Sorry if that sounds simplistic.'

'A lot of how our lives turn out comes down to where we are born, doesn't it?' There were the wild cards that life dealt when a person wasn't looking but luck did contribute to how and where he or she sorted out those problems.

'You think?' His eyes sparkled and his mouth lifted into a weary smile.

'I do.' She smiled back, enjoying the connection without her hormones doing their dance. Then her back gave a stab of pain, and she tightened up, held still.

'Hey, you okay?' His instant concern could undo her resolve not to give in to the attraction between them. 'You seem to be hurting more than usual.'

He noticed that pain struck her sometimes? 'I'm good. An injury I received in the army is playing up, that's all.' She gasped. She never, ever mentioned that, not even light-heartedly.

His concern deepened. 'Are you serious? Is that why you got out?'

She shook her head, wanting to deny the truth.

But she couldn't lie. 'I took an honourable discharge. My back acquired a dislike to humping around overweight packs and war gear.' She'd tried for light and friendly, thought she'd succeeded until she saw something in Chase's steady gaze that said he wasn't fooled. Something that drew her to tell him, 'I took a severe wound to my thigh and twisted my back. It's taking time but I'm coming right.' She turned towards her patient, needing to shut down this conversation.

Chase said softly, 'Glad to hear that, Kris.'

Her eyes closed and her head dipped. 'Kristina.'

He chuckled. 'Kristina.'

'You…' she spluttered as she turned back to him. 'You're deliberately winding me up.' She laughed, for real this time.

'Worth it to see your eyes widen as though I'd swiped one of your chocolate biscuits when you weren't looking.'

Which he had a penchant for.

As Kristina absorbed Chase's presence, her feet once again glued to the floor, the sparks that had flickered on and off between them since they'd met over Antoine suddenly became a raging fire in her veins. Worse, Chase was recognising her reaction.

Definitely time to put any dumb ideas about letting this attraction rule her head into the recycle bin. The only way to do that was to front up and explain she wasn't interested. In other words, lie her heart out. Tonight she'd do something about it, despite Chase never acknowledging the magnetism hovering between them. There were moments when he looked at her as though he wanted her. That was when her body really hummed; and her mind argued with it. Tonight she would not go to her bunk the moment she'd eaten dinner to get some sleep before the next draining shift began. No, she'd face up to Chase and deal with this annoying interference that crossed her day too often, sending her into an uncontrollable tailspin.

'Hey, Reid, how's things?' Chase settled his butt against the bulkhead of his private corner and stared out to sea, the phone hard against his ear.

'I'm good. You?'

Chase let out a long, satisfying breath. 'Another day almost done; more people helped, saved, fixed.' The relief was immense. He could rest easy—until the next day got under way. Ethan would understand where he was coming from. 'Not sure you're aware you left your tablet on board. I can send it out on the helicopter and have them courier it to you.'

'Keep it there till I come back. I don't need it

for the next couple of weeks. Claire doesn't leave me time for reading.' Ethan chuckled.

'Glad to hear she's keeping you on your toes.' Chase grinned, and couldn't deny the envy sweeping through him. 'You decided where you're going to look for work after you finish with us?'

'I've been talking to the local refugee centre. If there's a vacancy coming up in Marseille then I want my name on it.' Ethan filled him in on what he'd been doing since he and Claire had left *SOS Poseidon*.

Chase listened avidly, enjoying the camaraderie—something he hadn't known since he'd withdrawn from getting close to people after the loss of Nick. He was still hesitant about letting loose and talking about anything and everything, but every day over the past six weeks when Ethan had worked on board they'd inched closer and the tension had eased somewhat. He still wasn't ready to let go the guilt about not saving Nick. And until he did that Reid would never get close.

For a span of time, standing here in his own small zone, letting Reid in, he could almost accept he'd made up for the past, could almost believe he deserved a chance at a future. Almost. Until he hit the pillow and the memories came knocking, and Nick appeared in his head. Then he'd have to get out of bed to start over.

'Anyone special in your life?' Ethan asked. When Chase growled, he added sadly, 'Just learning about you. You know?'

Yeah, he knew. There was so much between them, and yet even more they hadn't a clue about. 'The answer to that should be obvious. There's no one for a very good reason.' Chase ignored the flare of pain. And the image of Kristina Morton that flashed into his mind. *She* might be as sexy as anything, but there was something about her that said don't touch unless you're serious. He was serious about having sex with her, but nothing more.

'So you're not interested in Kristina?'

Silence. He couldn't lie. Neither would he give Reid ammunition to give him a hard time.

Ethan sighed. 'She makes you laugh when no one else does. As for the sparks between the two of you, they had me looking for the fire extinguisher.'

Again Chase ignored him. Those comments were too close for comfort. If this was what having a friend was like, he didn't need one. Except over the previous six weeks he had begun to look forward to moments talking with Ethan. 'Nothing's going to come of those sparks. I'm all work and no play.' He already had parents and a sister who loved him and who he couldn't risk letting down—like he believed he had Nick even knowing he couldn't have changed a thing. The guilt did that to him. This getting a little friendlier with Reid didn't mean he was capable of allowing a woman close.

The breeze moved around him, fanning his face. 'Got to go. Talk to you again.'

Kristina slipped up beside him. Apparently she had no qualms about intruding into his private spot out here. From the first trip of the summer it had got around that this particular corner was his, and no one encroached. No one until tonight. Sure, he'd rung Ethan, and been relaxed about talking to him here, because it had been his choice. But… 'Kristina?'

The breeze also held that scent of pine and flowers. That sweet and spicy aroma went with her all over the ship. Sometimes it followed him into sleep at night. Those were the times he woke restless and in need of a cold shower.

Why did she invade his privacy like she had a right to? Funny how he couldn't find it in him to care. Instead, he felt unusually happy she'd joined him, a feeling he couldn't explain, neither was he about to try. It didn't mean he was letting her close. He hadn't lost all his faculties. They might've locked eyes over breakfast, sending the temperature in the room off the scale, but he'd had to deny the need boiling in his gut. Had to. How they'd walked away from each other was a mystery. *So send her away before it happened again.*

'Please, don't call me Kris.'

'Kristina. Got it.' That morning he'd kept crossing paths with her as they'd gone about their patients, and the tension in his body had wound tighter and tighter. Calling her Kris had been a deliberate wind-up. He'd thought she'd be angry, but instead she'd made him laugh.

'Good.'

'Other people must shorten your name.' There had to be a reason *Kris* upset her. She wasn't the type to be precious about her name. She carried herself with confidence and the upright stance common to military personnel. That poise kept everyone on their toes, including him, until one day on the last trip he'd seen a wealth of pain glittering in her eyes as they'd watched a child being buried at sea. Her tiny heart had given up within hours of coming on board—lack of food, too much sun, and who knew what else had taken the ultimate toll. It had been personally painful for him. Failing to save that girl despite doing everything possible and then some to bring her back to life had pained him.

He hadn't asked Kristina what was behind her agony. Things like that were too private to share. Hell, he was still getting used to the idea of him and Reid talking about the avalanche that had altered their lives for ever, and how Ethan had said they both had to learn to let go and move on. As if it was that easy. *It could be.* Oh, sure.

Leaning her elbows on the rail, Kristina stared out over the moonlit Mediterranean and breathed deeply, saying nothing.

A female who didn't talk the lid off a pot? Nothing like Libby, then. His sister never knew when to stop gabbing at him about why he should stop wandering the world and return home to be near the family. Chase sighed. He came out here for solitude while he went through his day and gave himself a pat on the back if he'd saved anyone. But right now he craved to hear Kristina's voice, couldn't bear this silence between them. He went with something innocuous. 'So you and Libby got on okay?'

'She makes the best blueberry muffins ever.' Kristina's head bobbed, and hair fell across her cheek. It was rare for her to let it free from the severe ponytail that was her signature style. Army style?

Many times over the past weeks he'd itched to flick the thick rope that fell down her back, pull away the band holding it in place to run his fingers through the golden waves. Shoving his fists deep into his pockets, he trawled his mind for something safe to say. 'What did you think of Merrywood?'

Kristina turned so the small of her back rested against the rail and a soft chuckle winded him with its warmth. 'I loved it. Everyone was so friendly and welcoming, I wanted to stay on.' Her fingers intertwined across her belly, tightening his gut further.

So much for playing safe. 'It can become claustrophobic, though. Especially when you're a teenager and don't want your parents finding out you've been smoking down by the river with your pals.'

There was a wistfulness in her eyes as she said, 'Surely that's part of belonging somewhere?'

Yep, and it tied a person to everyone so that when things went wrong they all were affected. Chase watched her hands making slow circular movements over her abdomen. Was she aware she did that whenever she went all thoughtful?

This time the urge to make her talk, to break down her barriers didn't bat him around the ears. Instead he relaxed, leaned against the rail, and went with being beside her, trying to accept this was as intimate as they should get. He had nothing to offer her other than a quick romp in the sack and they weren't doing that. He didn't trust this *thing* gripping him to let him go afterwards.

But Kristina was unlike any other woman who'd pressed his buttons. *She* pressed them hard. Could that be the reason for his restlessness? He wasn't in the market for a partner. Not when he had to be finding more people to save, trying to redeem himself for Nick. How many more lives would it take to be free of the guilt?

Chase pushed the past aside, took a deep breath. The air was soft and warm, not cooling as the sun dropped below the horizon. Summer warmed his skin and his soul. There'd been a year when he'd followed summer around the world, working in countries where snow and ice were alien, because he'd known how snow could destroy a person and he would never put himself in that position again.

But it hadn't been enough so he'd enrolled in med school to learn in earnest how to save people. London winters were cold but his heart had coped, had borne the pain that came with memories of a colder, icier, crueller place he'd never returned to. Not once. Never would. He couldn't. It wasn't in him to go there and bury the ghosts. They would never let him get away a second time. Except these past weeks, spending time with Reid, tentatively touching on what had happened, he'd begun looking at things in a different light. Would it be possible to put it all behind him one day?

Kristina's soft voice snagged him. 'I was called Kris in the army. When I wasn't sir or captain.' A tightness had crept into her tone.

'You let them?'

'Regardless of what the recruitment officers say, the military is still a masculine world. To fit in I was Kris. But I've objected to being called it since I was ten.'

'Am I allowed to ask why?'

'No big deal,' she answered in a harsh tone, suggesting it was. 'When my parents split up, my mother took me to LA with her where she met a man she was very keen on. When he proposed he told her in no uncertain terms that *Kris* was not part of the deal. The way he called me Kris was derogatory. I loathed it.'

Chase leaned closer, breathed deeply of her scent. He'd never call her Kris again. Not even as a tease. 'Did your mother tell him where to go?'

'No. I returned to England soon after.'

'To live with your father?'

'Dad was working twenty-four, seven trying to recoup the fortune he'd lost. I was sent to boarding school.'

'Geez.' She hadn't known the loving family environment he'd grown up with, had taken for granted, and now struggled not to put in danger by being near them. Lightly dropping his arm over her shoulders, Chase tucked her close. 'That's lousy.' A damned sight worse. His parents had stood by him through the days and years following the avalanche and still did. There'd been times they'd been so near he'd not been able to breathe, but he wouldn't have swapped that for what Kristina had missed out on. Yes, he was incredibly lucky to have such a loving, caring family.

'Yeah, it was.'

He daren't delve deeper, afraid she might sprint away, regret telling him in the first place. He didn't want her leaving his side, not until the tension in her stance softened and a smile returned to her eyes.

The silence returned, comfortable in an intimate way. Another first for him. The more he learned about this strong woman the more he wanted to know. Things like why she'd joined the army in the first place. Had she needed to belong to something, somewhere, to replace the lack of having a loving family around her? 'Were you ever deployed overseas?' He hadn't been going to ask any more questions so his words surprised him.

'I served in Brunei, where there are jungle warfare courses going on all the time.'

'I can't imagine being a soldier, charging around learning to kill people.' He shuddered. 'Not when my whole focus is on saving them.' Hell, she had *him* talking, wanting to tell her what made him tick. This was his time out, yet Kristina had sauntered into his space and *he* started gabbing on like he'd been on a desert island for months.

'It's not quite like that. I was a medic first and foremost. But sometimes I found myself questioning why I was there.'

'I'd be hopeless. Can't take orders from anyone.' Not since the day his skiing coach had dropped the ball when he'd been needed most. Coach Wheeler had phoned parents, tried to keep him from returning into the wrecked chalet, but he hadn't rushed in to help pull Nick free.

She turned under his arm and smiled up at him. 'Now, there's a surprise.'

He laughed, a belly-deep reaction that spread throughout his psyche. 'I know. Pig-headed is another term for the way I get things done.' Studying the sea, he asked, 'Do you miss the military life?'

'Not at all.' Her smile switched off. 'It wasn't what I wanted after all.' A little shiver and, 'See you in the morning.' Then she was gone, striding across the deck in that sharp, exact way of hers, heading for the hub of what went on day after day. Her leg left pulled a fraction higher on the upward movement. He'd noticed weeks ago how some days were worse than others, and how she sometimes winced or rubbed her lower back when she thought no one was looking. She wasn't one to complain or talk about her aches and pains.

She was back, a light smile on her face that heartened him. 'By the way, you'd make a lousy commanding officer.' Straightening, she mimicked him. 'Kristina, your attention—now.' This time she did leave him, flipping her hand over her shoulder on the way.

She left him chuckling yet bereft of company when he'd never before wanted anyone sharing this precious hour away from the cries and arguments and chatter that filled the ship twenty-four seven. Sometimes his head would be splitting apart with everyone's pain, his own grief and guilt working its way into the centre of it all, reminding him why he was there, and stressing that he'd never be able to escape to a normal life back in England close to his family. He had to continue moving, keep finding more people to save. Working for MFA did that by bringing him and those people together. Day after day, week after week. There was no end to it. And not likely to be for the rest of his life. Which suited him perfectly.

Except Kristina didn't recognise his barriers, or ignored them, relentlessly chipping away, making him feel a little happier with life. Hell, he'd put his arm around her to give her warmth and support. Something more than her beauty, her confidence, her quietness, her heat-provoking body got to him—come on, it was a combination of all those.

Yeah, but there was an indefinable something else he couldn't put his finger on. When she'd told him about her name he'd known instantly she didn't talk about that to anyone, yet she'd told him. Not to shut him up, or at least not to let him think it was on a whim, but because she'd wanted him to understand there were heartfelt reasons behind her need to be called Kristina. She'd even told him those. Information he didn't want because it made him care. From now on he was done talking to her about anything deep. He had to be or he was doomed.

Chase tried to connect the dots between the doctor and her role as a soldier. Though the circumstances were poles apart, the requirements for patience and tolerance would be the same, yet he couldn't quite imagine Kristina issuing orders. Around here other medics did her bidding without question, her manner friendly and relaxed while underscored with determination, but a military officer would have to be sharp and firm. Bet she filled out the uniform perfectly.

Hell, he was in need of some diversion. Last time he'd got like this a nurse had spent a night with him on their three-day leave from the ship. Eight months ago, at the end of last summer. That was the last time he'd had sex? So it wasn't sleep he needed, was it?

CHAPTER TWO

So much for confronting Chase about the frustrating attraction going on between them. Kristina stared at the bunk above her. Damn, but she was tired, kept awake by the shock that she'd wanted to take a risk and throw herself at him as they'd stood in the quiet of his corner. That she'd so nearly thrown aside her protective barriers and plastered herself against that sexy body, known every last inch of him, felt him take her deep. So, so close.

How could that happen when she'd gone to tell him they had to get past whatever it was between them? She hadn't gone to make it worse, stronger, *real*.

Because Chase had got her talking about herself. That was almost sexy, being something she didn't do. Like laying herself out naked in front of him, telling him personal stuff was as intimate. At least she hadn't mentioned her guilt, how a man had died on her watch. That would've been a passion killer—exactly what she'd gone to him to do. Damn, but her head space was a mess.

She'd nearly thrown herself at him. But it was all right. She hadn't. Somehow she'd managed to step away, with a smile even. But she had turned back, fighting the need to leave and the greater need to stay. To risk everything. It was that risk that had caught up with her at the last moment and made her come out with the nonsense about him not making a good officer.

If only she hadn't. Glad she had. How had she done it? When her feet had been aimed in his direction, her blood thickening with desire, her fingers tense with the need to touch his skin? Guess looking out for herself was so ingrained it worked regardless of where her body wanted to go.

Kristina swallowed her confusion and rolled off the bottom bunk to stand hunched over, biting her bottom lip as pain jarred her back.

'You all right?' Jane, her cabin mate, asked from above.

'These bunks must've been designed by a sadist.' Knuckling her lower back, she began the ritual of straightening up, slowly easing tension from the muscles, not giving in to their stabbing protests. Then her left thigh got in on the act, shooting pain up into her butt.

'I wouldn't know. When my head hits the pillow I'm gone.'

Kristina's laugh was tight. 'I heard.' There'd been a lot of snoring going on during the night.

A pair of legs swung over the side of the bunk and Jane sat up, rubbing her eyes. 'What's with your back anyway? I often see you pummelling it.'

She gave her usual answer, not the one she'd told Chase. *Gave too much away there.* 'I haven't been doing the yoga exercises that keep me nimble.' No time or unpopulated space for those.

'Borrow Chase's bolthole when he's not around.'

Right, and be on guard in case he turned up? That would negate the purpose of yoga. He went there at some point every night. The plan was to turn Chase back into a man she could talk to about everyday things, not the deep or ugly, then walk away without a backward glance. Not a man to get hot and edgy around. 'There's little room for stretching.'

'That's a shame.'

No, it was a relief. 'Isn't it?' Getting into Downward Facing Dog with Chase watching would have her heart going ballistic. And who knew what the sight of her backside poking skywards would do for him? He might be disgusted, but she doubted it. The physical friction between them that she'd done nothing to stop screamed attraction, intense and exciting and getting stronger; the mental not so much. He liked to be in control of everything around him, probably had to be since he was SARCO.

Would he be like that in bed? His guard had dropped while they'd talked last night. That hour had been comfortable in a way she'd not known with any man. As though the friction had been on hold, allowing room for getting to know each other on a different level. He'd been understanding about why she didn't want to be called Kris, and she'd swear he'd nearly laughed when she'd taken the mickey out of him over calling her to attention.

There was more to the man than she'd discovered so far. Lots more, and what she wouldn't do to learn it all. Perhaps she should've gone the other way last night and dragged him along to his cabin and put these feelings to rest in the only way possible.

Oh, no, you don't. House and job in the burbs, remember?

Jane's feet hit the floor with a thud. 'I need a long, hot shower, then I'm going to try for some more sleep.' All she'd get was short, wet and cool in the shower box.

'Me, too, for the shower.' Kristina tugged clean underwear and a white T-shirt with the MFA logo and shorts from her pack. The simple dress code was a bonus. Dressing for the locum role wasn't so bad, but as for the army uniform, she never wanted to see another, let alone wear one. That'd taken her desire to fit in and belong to a whole new level. She hadn't belonged, she'd been submerged.

The knee-length shorts she shook out hid the scar running down her thigh to avoid the questions that'd invariably come when someone got an eyeful. Explaining that being thrown through the air by a bomb blast to land on a steel girder that had rendered her incapacitated wasn't happening. Not when it had meant she'd been unable to save Corporal Higgs from bleeding out, though it was unlikely he'd have survived anyway. She'd cried with frustration and despair until medics back at HQ had administered drugs that had taken her under. Unfortunately the drugs hadn't conquered her guilt.

A training exercise had gone hideously wrong that day, changing her for ever, altering the direction she'd been taking in an attempt to find the equivalent of family. The military wasn't it. People within the units were close, caring, and always had each other's backs, but something had been missing, something she'd spent most of her life looking for. Boarding school hadn't been able to make up for the loving family environment she'd known for the first decade of her life, neither had med school. Now she knew better, had grown up some, and understood she had to be comfortable in her own skin before anyone could share her life. She'd touched on that at Merrywood, enough to start believing it was possible.

Jane appeared in her misty line of vision. 'The showers are empty at the moment. Just saying, you know?'

'Thanks.'

When she arrived at breakfast, Chase was the only person there. 'Hey, where is everyone?' she asked.

'It's not six yet.'

Then they'd have a few minutes to themselves. That filled her with warmth when she should be taking her breakfast out onto the deck—alone. With a plate of scrambled eggs and toast cook had just put up, Kristina strolled across to sit at a table with him instead, unable to resist spending a few minutes alone with him. 'Have you done a round of our patients yet?'

'I've seen the earache boy this morning. Dad slept the night on the floor beside him and was very amenable towards me, all thanks to you, I reckon.'

The father of a young boy had been having trouble letting anyone near his son, mainly because he'd been exhausted and struggling to cope with where he was. 'Guess I got lucky.' She wouldn't mind getting lucky with this man.

Thought I was supposed to get over him. 'Or the father was tiring and needed someone to indicate what to do next.'

'You don't accept compliments easily, do you?'

She shrugged. 'Wasn't aware of it.'

'I'll have to give you some more.' He laughed. He was doing that a lot lately around her.

More warmth flowed over her skin. How was she supposed to walk away from this? Forking food into her mouth, she tried to make sense of what was happening to her. The eggs were dry and the toast soft. But her mind was on high alert. So she was admitting she felt something for Chase? Chew, swallow. Try some more, wash it down with tea. She couldn't feel anything for Chase. Mustn't. Wanted to.

Chase asked, 'What did you do in Barcelona, by the way? I hardly ever saw you at our hotel.'

Like he'd been hanging around, joining in with everyone. And she'd been looking. 'It was Barcelona.' She gave a strangled laugh. 'Shopping, tapas, shopping, wine. I was with Collette and Rani, and they made my shopping attempts look pathetic.' At the end of the three days the two nurses had come back to the ship laden with bags. 'I also took a day trip to the Pyrenees, driving through stunning countryside along the way. It was all a bit rushed so I'd like to go there again for longer.' It had taken her away from the city and stopped her incessant scanning for this man.

'Spain's spectacular. I spent time there before I started my training. Surfing, jet-skiing, diving. All good fun.'

So he hadn't always been focused on nothing but patients and helping people. 'Time off before the real world took over.'

His hand tightened around his fork, and his face took on a strained look. 'Something like that.'

Wanting his smile back, she leaned over and stole a piece of his bacon. 'You emptied the dish, you've got to share.'

'Hey, first in and all that.' The strain disappeared.

Feeling so much happier, she stabbed another piece on his plate, held it at her mouth as she said, 'Pierre can't have cooked much if you got the last of it.'

'Keep this up and I'll hardly taste bacon.'

'Now you come to mention it.' She held her fork over his plate again.

Chase whipped his breakfast out of reach. 'I don't think so.'

'You want tea?' She rose from the table. 'Or coffee?'

'Coffee. Milk and one.' Then he glinted at her

through eyes that seemed to see right inside her. 'Sugar, not salt.'

'Spoilsport.' She put the salt shaker back on the counter, and spooned sugar into a mug. 'Wonder how high the temperature's going to reach today. Yesterday was a scorcher.' A dollop of ice would help right now, tipped down the front of her T-shirt. Her body was steaming, all because of Chase, sitting there looking hot and yummy.

'The forecast's saying low thirties.' Chase looked happy. Not an ice man, then? 'I like the heat,' he added before she could ask.

Placing his coffee on the table, she sipped her tea and studied him, in particular those muscles shaping the front of his loose T-shirt. Those dark curls falling all over his head needed shaping, too—with her fingers. She gripped her mug with both hands. Lowered her gaze to the light stubble darkening his chin. Tightened her grip further. Rubbing her palm over his face would really quieten the thrumming of her blood. 'Just as well considering the countries MFA takes you to.'

'I guess.' He was watching her. What did he see? Not the guilt, the pain, the need to be settled, please. Try happy, fun, lovable.

'Seems you two were up early.' Calvin strolled into the room. 'Pierre, can we have some more eggs and bacon out here?' he called through the hatch into the galley. 'These two haven't left any-thing.'

Kristina felt her smile shifting, away from Chase and into a general one. Their brief moment alone together was over for the day.

'I've scheduled you with me this morning,' Chase told her. 'There're a number of patients with fuel burns that require debridement. There's one young man whose injuries are particularly disturbing.' He placed his mug back on the table and turned it round and round between his fingers, his gaze now fixed on the depths of milky coffee, his meal forgotten.

She nudged him, ignored the force of heat where her elbow contacted his arm. 'Eat up. You've got a full day to get through.'

'You're right.' Picking up his fork, he took a mouthful of egg and swallowed it without chewing.

'Food is a tool to keep going, no matter what's thrown at us.' The eggs weren't wonderful. Not even a heavy dousing of salt helped, and probably only aggravated their BPs. 'What time's the first patient scheduled?'

'As soon as we're done here.' There he went again, tilting his mouth into that fascinating smile. As though he'd shoved away whatever was bothering him and wanted to continue enjoying this break between patients and more patients without worrying about how to help them.

'Why me and not Abdul?'

'You're saying you don't want to help me?' A tightness entered his voice and turned his face into a scowl.

'Chase.' She tapped the back of his hand. No heat this time. 'That's not what I asked. But think about it. I'm a GP. Abdul might be insulted if I do his work.'

The tightness backed off, the scowl smoothed into a small smile. 'He's catching up on sleep after a long night doing minor ops. The last boat-load we picked up came with a list of minor surgeries as long as my leg.'

Her gaze immediately dropped to his long, muscular legs with their tanned skin. She drank in the sight. *Get over yourself. They're legs. Everyone has them.* Yeah, but— She gulped her tea.

This was ridiculous. Chase's focus was firmly on helping those less fortunate, not on her. He was a man about whom no one on board had any grizzles. A regular guy doing extraordinary things to make life more comfortable for others. This attraction must've come from spending so much time in confined quarters surrounded by too many people. Like in the army when soldiers were jam-packed into bunkers for endless hours, watching for the enemy. Those times had always tested her patience. This growing need to get intimate with the most breathtakingly good-looking man she'd ever known would evaporate as soon as her contract was over—in a little over five weeks. An eternity.

What would it be like to leave the ship with him and go home? She wasn't going to know. She didn't have a place to call home, and when she did Chase would still be trotting around the globe.

How could her mind wander when Chase was still talking? But she'd been thinking about him, not the medical arena he was discussing. Time to focus on the practical, not the impossible. 'Right, I'll get ready for surgery.'

Surely the attraction vibes would shut up in the medical room where concentration on the operation and the patient was paramount?

Her hormones didn't get that message, sending heat zipping around her veins as she stood in the medical corner where they were working, listening to Chase explain which wounds they were to debride and which to leave.

'I'm concerned about infection, and working on every little wound will make him very vulnerable to bacteria.' Those strong hands described in fluid movements what they'd soon be doing to their patients. What would they feel like on her breasts? 'The larger wounds are going to be trouble enough.'

'Will you send him off with plenty of antibiotics and painkillers?' Chase dressed in blue, baggy cotton scrubs did nothing to quieten the excitement going on over her skin, in her moist places.

'Enough to get him through this crisis.'

In the meantime they'd do their best to counteract infection while the man was with them. She reached for the gloves and winced as her back protested. Definitely time to find somewhere to do a few stretches. Not on the open deck at the front when Chase could appear at any moment she was in her zen zone.

Chase peered at her. 'Back bothering you?'

About to die of embarrassment if he'd read her mind, she snapped, 'Just a twinge.' It was better when he hadn't noticed. Until Chase had asked yesterday she'd never mentioned her injuries to anyone on board, not even when filling in her application to work for MFA. So she'd fudged the truth, but it wasn't as though it caused problems for others, such as covering her shifts. Besides, the injuries were improving, though slower than she would have liked.

'Right, we'll get started.' The shoulder he turned in her direction wasn't cold, neither was it warm and friendly.

She'd let him down by not sharing. 'I'm okay, truly.'

He glanced across. 'I have some massage experience if that'd help.' Then he straightened, shock registering in his face. 'I mean…'

Chase lost for words? It would've been funny if she wasn't feeling equally flustered. 'It's fine.' She shoved her hand into a glove with such force it split. 'I'll do some yoga later.'

'Here.' Chase held out the box of gloves. 'The offer stands if you change your mind.' He'd obviously got a grip on himself faster than she had.

'Thanks,' she muttered, turning to the table where their man lay, mouth open, snoring softly. Thank goodness for patients. Kristina picked up a scalpel and began cutting away the infected skin around a large wound on the right leg.

'Yoga, eh?' There he went again. Grinning like she amused him.

'Don't laugh until you've tried it,' she retorted through a smile.

Nearly an hour later Kristina stood back from the table. 'He is going hurt when he wakes up.'

'Morphine will help for a while, followed by strong painkillers. Hopefully those wounds will be healing before he leaves us.' Chase dropped the scalpel he'd used into a metal dish. The clatter was sharp in the stuffy room.

The next patient was wheeled across and they were away again.

'The air-conditioning gone on the blink?' Kristina wondered aloud as they finished debriding their fourth patient. Over the last thirty minutes the room had become hot enough to keep a mug of tea warm.

'Seems like it.' Chase snapped off his gloves and tossed them in the direction of the hazardous waste bin. 'Anyone for a quick coffee on the outer deck before lunch?'

'Definitely,' the anaesthetist said.

'Not me. I'll check how the vaccinations are going.' It'd take all day and half the night to get all one hundred and something people inoculated. Chase would have it covered, but she had to get away from him, breathe clear air into her lungs and not the kind that was tainted with Chase scent. Male, sharp, sometimes abrasive, sometimes seductive. Definitely mind-blowing. And disruptive.

'See you at lunch,' Chase grumped.

'Maybe,' she gave back.

In the end, Kristina decided to avoid Chase and took some sandwiches back to her cabin where she squashed her yoga mat in the narrow gap between the bunk and the wall. Sitting with her legs crossed at the ankles and her hands on her knees, she tried not to bang her elbows and closed her eyes to begin clearing her mind of everything. Taking slow breaths deep into her belly, holding, relaxing, gradually the tension in her aching muscles let go, and she was able move freely. She began a workout of simple positions, allowing her mind to drift and her body to mend.

Placing her hands on the floor and pushing her butt upward, keeping her legs straight, Kristina hung her head between her arms. So relaxing, so freeing. When no one was staring at her butt, that was, and in here she could be sure of that.

Chase Barrington strolled through her head like he had every right to be there.

Forget relaxed. Her body became a temple to tension. Every last muscle tightened. Dropping to her knees, she stared at the mat under her hands. Damn him. Why couldn't he leave her alone for once? All the good work had come undone in a flash. There wasn't time for any more. She should've been in the clinic ten minutes ago. Hauling herself upright, she dumped the mat on her bunk and headed out the door. At least her back and thigh felt better.

The same couldn't be said for her head space. Chase had settled in, and wasn't taking a blind bit of notice of her need for a clear mind.

He also had ideas about her next job. 'Kristina, could you examine Marjali? Zala says there's blood between her legs.'

Back up to speed, she answered, 'Hopefully it's normal post-partum bleeding. Zala mightn't know about that.' Slipping on gloves, she looked around. 'I'll talk to them, see if I am allowed to do an examination.'

'You will be.' Chase sounded so certain she turned to stare at him.

'There's no guarantee. We're the strangers in this situation.'

The shade of Chase's eyes lightened to summer and the corners of his mouth lifted. 'I wouldn't place a bet on this. I'd hate to take advantage of you.'

His belief in her ability to get along with a woman who lived such a different life startled her. It also lightened her heart, made her feel good. 'I promise not to deliberately skew the outcome of my discussion with Marjali just to prove you wrong.'

Wow. When Chase put a bit of effort into it his smile could light up the world. It certainly brightened hers, and she forgave him for crowding her head space. But she left him before she got carried away with this feeling of wonder and said or did something they'd both regret.

'Zala, help me pull these curtains around Marjali, will you?'

Zala grabbed a handful of curtain to tug along the metal rail. 'Is this right?'

'Yes. Now I have questions for you to ask Marjali.' Kristina drew a breath as she thought about how to word them in a way Zala would understand clearly to translate, and how Marjali would understand her intentions. 'Tell her I need to look at where the blood is coming from.'

'It's where the baby was,' Zala looked at her as though she was stupid.

'You are right, but sometimes after a baby there can be too much. Do you understand?' She had to or this wasn't going any further.

Zala gave an abrupt nod before talking to the other woman in a low, urgent voice, pointing at Kristina and then at the top of Marjali's legs.

Marjali regarded Kristina with a surprising intensity, her almost black eyes drilling right into her. Finally she nodded.

'You can look,' Zala informed her with satisfaction. 'I told her you are nice.'

Blink, blink. Really? Lifting her arms, she made to hug Zala, hesitated. Again she wasn't sure if it was acceptable. 'Thank you.'

Zala leaned in and put her hand on Kristina's wrist. 'It is good, yes?'

'Yes, it's good. Please tell Marjali everything I say.' Explaining in simple terms what she was doing, Kristina quickly found the source of bleeding. A tear had occurred since the birth. 'I am going to give her an injection.' Then she'd stitch the tear.

'Injection?'

'A needle to stop it hurting.'

Collecting the suture kit and drawing up a small dose of local painkiller, Kristina returned to the bed. Zala's explanation had gone down well. Within a short time everything was done and Marjali was sitting up.

'Slowly,' Kristina warned. 'What have you been doing since baby was born?'

'She's been carrying buckets of water to the men.'

'She's not to do that. That's why she was bleeding. There are other people to lift the buckets.' If any of the medics had seen Marjali hauling water around they'd have intervened, not that they'd necessarily be taken notice of. 'Tell her it's important to rest.' There might've been previous babies, but the woman wasn't in top health.

'I tell her.'

'What was Marjali's problem?' Chase asked as Kristina dumped her gloves, the used syringe and cotton pads in the waste.

'She's been hauling water containers around the deck when I thought she was resting with her baby.'

'Not any more she's not,' Chase growled. 'I'll talk to the man overseeing this group.'

'Maybe don't use Zala to translate that one. It might be seen as a female stepping into the men's shoes.'

'Good point.' Chase touched her lightly on the shoulder. A gesture that made her heart squeeze.

How could she close down these feelings for him? They were growing into more than attraction, more than the need to just have sex with him. But making love would be a great start.

Kristina put her plate in the dishwasher. 'That's it. I'll go and see Marjali and the baby then head to my bunk,' she said to the room in general. It was after nine. Dinner had been quiet, everyone lost in their own exhaustion.

'You're not going topside, then?' Jane asked quietly.

'No need. I did a few yoga moves in our cabin earlier.'

'I wasn't thinking about yoga.' The woman had the cheek to wink.

Jane knew she'd been up there with Chase last night? Why was she surprised? The gossip mill spun well in the confined places crowded with people having nothing better to occupy their minds. Everyone required a diversion from their work at one time or another. If only it wasn't her. 'I'll be in our cabin.'

Marjali was asleep, her baby swathed in a cotton sheet in a crib beside her. Reluctant to disturb either of them, Kristina stood watching over them for a few minutes. Such an unimaginable place to be, and yet the woman had had a baby and was getting on with being a mother. Not that she had any choice, Kristina sighed. At least *she* did. Starting with finding her next job—preferably in another Merrywood, if not the real deal. The more she thought about the quaint town the more she wanted to be a part of it. Merrywood had firmly lodged in her heart.

Stepping outside into fresh air and the light breeze that had come up, she wandered around the crowded space. The noise was continuous and blocked her thinking. The idea of retreating to the stuffy cabin no longer appealed. Which left only one place that might be quiet, cool and empty. Except for one person, and he knew how to be silent without creating a strain on her.

'I wondered if you'd come,' Chase said as she slipped in beside him and propped her elbows on the railing, making sure there was a gap between them.

Touching him was not an option. It wouldn't shut down the lure of his body. 'I needed some quiet time.'

'Then I won't ask what you're thinking about,' he said around one of those devastating smiles she'd started looking out for, and seemed to find more and more often.

'Work, as in where to next,' she told him, because he was far too easy to talk to.

'You want to return home.'

'Yes.' They weren't meant to be talking. Even if it was what she needed after all. He'd send her away. He'd started it, though.

'Pity.' He moved sideways a little, away from her, leaving her feeling she'd made a blunder. 'You're just what we need around here.'

As SARCO Chase gave more than most. Not everyone could be expected to do the same. 'If one percent of the medical profession gave six or twelve weeks out of their careers to work for *Medicine For All* there'd be an over-supply of staff.'

'Unfortunately it doesn't work like that,' Chase answered. 'What are you looking for this time?'

'I'd prefer a permanent position in a small town medical centre. But it's not as easy as I'd hoped,' she sighed. 'Merrywood spoiled me for choice. All the staff were welcoming and friendly. It was the same with the townsfolk.' Going to the pub for a drink on a Saturday had been relaxing and enjoyable, with people coming up to talk to her like she was a local. Now all she had to do was find something similar to make permanent and she was home and settled.

What about the love interest she'd started longing for? A man to come home to at the end of the day to share a drink and meal with while talking about what they'd done was a dream that slotted into the picture of family she'd waited for since her real family had fallen apart. The hazy memories of being hugged after school, taken out for a walk with the dog, being helped with her homework never quite disappeared, and always tugged at her, filled her with longing for another chance at that life.

Kristina's eyes moved sideways, towards Chase. Damn but he was gorgeous. Dragging her gaze forward again, she stared at the waters below. Dark and dangerous. Her gaze returned to the man beside her. His head was tipped slightly back and his eyes were closed. His hands lightly held the railing and his legs were splayed to counteract the rolling of the ship on the low swell. Dark and dangerous? Maybe. Intriguing and exciting, for sure. Was this what she wanted in a man?

CHAPTER THREE

'REID, I'M CHECKING you're joining us aboard the *Poseidon* for the three weeks.' The man was busy with planning a wedding and finding a house to buy, Chase allowed.

'I gave you my word.' The underlying note in Ethan's tone told him that when he promised something he didn't go back on it.

'Sorry,' Chase admitted. He'd said that a lot lately. Ethan and Kristina had a knack of making him say things without thinking them through first. 'It's not you I'm worried about. People are pulling out of contracts and others getting ill so the roster I worked out before summer has gone to pieces.'

'Afraid I can't do more time or Claire will hang me out to rot. Though I'm really over choosing between lace or satin. And that's for the place settings at the wedding party we're having later on.'

Chase relaxed and laughed. 'I like it that Claire can wind you up.' His laughter died. He'd never have that. There was no one to blame but himself. He'd chosen the solitary road.

Yet lately there'd been occasions, especially since he and Ethan had begun burying the hatchet, when he'd give anything to forget the past and move on to something exciting and loving that could span his whole future. A relationship, a marriage with rock-solid foundations, so that there were kids and a home to be proud of and go back to at the end of every day.

Kristina came to mind. He shoved her away. First he had to stop holding onto his guilt over having to let Nick die alone. It had taken a crane to lift the beam from Nick's chest the day after the avalanche had struck. While in Chase's head he knew what that meant, in his heart he couldn't quite reconcile himself with the truth. What would happen if he did relax on the guilt? Would the sky fall in? *Nick? Would you think I'd deserted you again?*

Ethan was muttering something.

Chase refocused. 'What did you say?'

'Being with Claire's taking some getting used to.' Ethan laughed. 'But I wouldn't change a thing.'

'Thank goodness she's stronger than you. She turned your head when you thought you had everything under control.'

'Don't get too wise, friend. The same could

happen to you when you're least expecting it. How is Kristina, by the way?'

Chase winced. That was getting a little too close to the mark. 'She's good, as are Freja, Pierre, Mike, and Angel.'

'You might be fooling yourself, Chase, but you're not fooling me. The pair of you need your heads banged together. Six weeks and all that tiptoeing around as though you weren't remotely interested in each other, the air pulsing with electricity. Damned dangerous for anyone getting near. Kristina gets under your skin and you're not liking it.'

'Time I got back to sorting out the roster. I'll mark you as definite for the next three-week stint.' He already had. This call really had nothing to do with that and all to do with talking with this man who was rapidly becoming a friend—if he stopped giving him crap about Kristina. All part of letting go of the past, surely?

'You know the routine. I'll email the exact date for embarking. Catch you.' There were volunteers doing three-, six-, nine- and twelve-week hauls. It would be a lot easier if everyone signed up for the same length of time, but that wasn't how the system worked.

'Chase, don't hang up,' Ethan shouted. 'Forget your bloody roster. What's this call really about?'

About to hit 'off', Chase hesitated. It had

taken too many years for them to start burying the things they'd said on that mountain for him to be stirring up more trouble. Losing ground wasn't an option. He had stopped blaming Reid for something he'd had no choice about—a huge step forward. Ethan now accepted Chase didn't hate him for surviving when Nick hadn't. Chase also understood the guilt he'd put on Ethan by letting him believe he'd made a choice between the two guys. Nick had never been coming out of there alive. *Nick, help me here.* Nothing but silence. The laden quiet he'd learned to live with, that crippled him.

Fill the hush. Try answering Reid honestly. Take a deep lungful and just say it. 'I wanted to touch base.' Reid would understand how big that was. They'd both admitted they'd avoided close friendships since that horrendous night, and that they weren't used to having someone to call just for the hell of it.

'You don't have to make up excuses to get in touch,' the man on the other end of the phone growled.

Chase grimaced. 'I'm still getting used to this.'

'You and me both.'

'Bet Claire doesn't let you go quiet on her.'

'Not a chance.'

How did that feel? Good? Frightening? Exciting? Kristina came to mind. Again. She did that way too often. What would it be like to give up this life and make a new one? With her? *Go away.* 'How are you finding this no more disappearing over the horizon at any moment thing?' He needed to know. For future reference, in case he ever decided to take a chance on a relationship. *Go away, Kristina.*

'There are moments when the fear grabs me and I start to tap into sites for jobs in the heat.' Ethan went quiet.

And this was summer, no snow and ice. But Ethan was in France. Where he'd sworn never to return. Chase waited. The last thing he wanted was to say something glib. They were better than that now.

Finally Ethan continued in a subdued voice. 'Then I look at Claire and know I don't want to go. That staying here, with her, is all I want, need, look forward to every morning in that split second between waking and opening my eyes to find her beside me. She's worth everything. Including being at the bottom of a mountain.'

Chase swallowed hard. Then had to do it again. 'I'm glad.' One of them had finally got their life back on track. Was it possible to make that two out of two? Fear rose; sharp and solid. What if he had to choose between the woman he loved and someone else in another emergency? He couldn't do it. He couldn't. So he wouldn't put himself in that position. *Sorry, Kristina.*

There was a lot of throat clearing going on at the other end. 'I want you to be my best man at our marriage ceremony.'

Chase felt his legs soften. Dropping his butt onto the desk top, he took the weight off his boneless limbs. Best man? With their past? This spoke volumes about how far they'd come in a short time. It spoke of total forgiveness. He couldn't find it within him to be flippant, his usual way of dealing with difficult, emotional moments. This was do or deny. Working with Ethan, he'd learned he didn't want denial any more. Not with this man. They'd been through hell together, the outcome taken out of their hands by a larger force. Now they were taking tentative steps towards a real, honest friendship and he wouldn't be the one to screw that. 'I'd be honoured.'

He might now be able to work at dropping the denial on living a settled life in one place with one woman. Huh? Too soon. Way too soon. He still had to steady himself over his friendship with Reid.

'Cut the fancy words,' Ethan croaked. '"Yes" would've been fine.'

'Send me the details. When's this happening?' The last wedding he'd been to had been when Libby had married Jarrod, her childhood sweetheart, and they now had a posse of kids that would drive an army commander to drink. Army. Kristina. The two words clashed and melded in his head. Would he ever get her out of there again? Had he transferred his denial from Ethan to her? Now, *that* was getting complex. Forget it.

'A month after the *Poseidon* ties up at the end of summer. Hope that won't mess with your plans for heading out to Africa.'

The contract lay in his in-box. He hadn't been able to bring himself to sign it. Every time this past week when he'd thought he'd print it off to scrawl his signature across the bottom, Kristina's beautiful face had slipped into his mind, and he'd put it off. But the day was coming when he'd have no choice. Liam had already emailed to ask where the contract was. All that had done was remind Chase how unlike him it was to dither. He'd do it today. It wasn't as though he was changing his career path because of Kristina.

'You still there?' Ethan asked.

'I'll be available for the wedding. No matter what turns up.'

'Thanks, Chase. It's not a wedding. We're getting married in the Marseille Town Hall, just the four of us there. Then we'll have big bash back at the family's village later on.'

'Four?' His stomach was tightening.

'Better warn you, Claire's asking Kristina to

be her bridesmaid.' He laughed as though that was the biggest joke of the week.

'You're winding me up.'

'Not much.' Ethan was still laughing. 'Catch you.' He was gone.

Chase stared at the phone, ready to hurl it across the room. He and Kristina were going to be beside Ethan and Claire as they publicly declared their love for each other. They were being pushed together, want it or not. Considering how well the two women got on, he should've realised this would happen. Apparently Claire didn't have lots of friends, or at least none she wanted to stand beside her more than Kristina. And she was searching for permanency in her life, making him the wrong man for her. Unless he followed in Reid's footsteps.

Impossible or terrifying? Both.

'Chase, the next load of refugees is alongside.' Kristina stood in the doorway, hands on delectable hips, looking amused.

Had she heard his end of the conversation with Ethan? Or had she already been talking to Claire and knew they'd both be going to the wedding—as partners, no less? 'You heard from Claire today?'

Her brow creased. 'No. Should I have?'

He'd put his large foot in it again. 'Ethan mentioned she might be phoning you, that's all.'

Standing up, he slipped the phone into his pocket, though there wasn't anyone else he wanted to hear from today. 'Let's go deal with our new patients.'

Then he'd be able to focus on what was necessary and ignore the rest.

Kristina wiped her face with tissues. They came away sodden. 'This heat is unbearable.'

'Be glad you're not on land.' Chase put his empty water bottle aside. 'There's a heatwave going on in Greece, Italy and southern France, with temperatures hitting the low forties in some areas.'

'How do people cope? I prefer the cold.'

Chase shivered. 'I don't.'

'Then again, when I've had to walk through snow and ice on my way to work I wished for the heat.' She grinned.

'No pleasing you, then.' His breathing was rapid, his smile forced.

'I used to enjoy snowboarding, whenever I had a chance to get up to the mountains, but it's been years since I gave it go. I'd probably make a right idiot of myself if I tried now.'

'Not my idea of fun.' There was something wrong about his tone, like she'd pushed the wrong buttons, upsetting him.

Yet she persisted. 'You've given it a go, then?'

'Not snowboarding.' He wasn't giving much away. All part of the 'don't talk a lot' in their quiet space on deck?

To her it was *their* place now. Over the past eight days she'd joined Chase every night for time out and not once had he told her to go away. It was special and she looked forward to being with him, to the lack of expectations put on her to fill in the minutes unless she wanted to. 'That's a yes to skiing?'

'It was a long time ago,' he muttered. The tension that had been tightening his arms and shoulders increased.

Desperate to undo the damage, she said the first thing that came into her mind. 'I don't like clothes that are remotely green or tan.'

His nod was short. 'I get that.'

'Heavy boots are no longer in my wardrobe either.'

One corner of his mouth lifted. 'Replaced with ten-inch high heels?'

'Ah, no. I fall off those too easily.'

'I'm disappointed.' He turned and leaned back against the rail, his gaze fixed on her now. 'I still can't get my head around you, so feminine and kind and fun, in the army. Why did you enlist?'

She should've stuck to the unspoken no-talking rule: instead, that sense of reaching for Chase, of feeling close to him, had got the better of her and now she was in the firing line. Looking out to sea, she wanted to tell him to leave her alone, wanted to put him back in the box where all people getting close went before they could hurt her by dumping her first. But something held her back. The need to find that future she wanted.

While Chase didn't stack up when it came to settling down, there was no denying he was helping her find her way. Telling him why she'd chosen the military couldn't hurt, might even help her get past the pain she carried into every relationship. 'I was looking for somewhere to belong.'

He studied her for a long time, before asking quietly, 'Did you find it?'

'Not really. This will sound weird to someone who comes from a loving family…' She paused, collecting the right words. 'Libby was always talking about her and Jarrod and the kids, and about your parents and you. She made it sound wonderful, having people behind you all the time no matter what you did.' Reminded her of her childhood.

'That's our Libby.' He sighed. 'She's not always right about everything.'

Kristina nodded. 'Who is?' Of course he didn't answer. There really wasn't one. Her gaze returned to the sea. There was anonymity in the heaving water and the hidden depths. 'I had this idea that being a part of the army would be on a

par to belonging to a family.' She daren't look at
Chase for fear there'd be mockery in his eyes. 'I
wanted someone to have my back, to feel I belonged with them. I got all of that.' It still wasn't
what she'd been hoping for.

'Where did it let you down?'

Chase got it. Again she watched him as she
talked, basking in his ability to be non-judgemental,
at least until he had all the facts.

'I *was* part of a dedicated group of people,
working, training, playing together, and it appeared to be exactly what I'd been hoping for.
Then I came to realise everything was on the
army's terms, as it has to be. Going into battle
as individuals would be disastrous. Every soldier
has to be, and is, integral to each other.'

Then she had been discharged and the gate had
closed firmly behind her. Bye-bye, Captain Morton. The two women she kept in touch with felt
the same sense of being left out in the cold once
they were no longer a part of the establishment,
though they all agreed that could be their own
fault because they'd expected too much.

'You obviously don't regret your decision despite not finding the right job yet.'

Again it sounded as though he understood
where she was coming from. Just like that. With
no follow-up questions about why, where and
when. That earned him a lot of points. Other

people like her father, who wasn't close by any
stretch of the imagination, hadn't believed the
truth, even knowing why she'd left the forces.
Her mother had never understood her need to
be loved for the person she was and not who her
mum wanted her to be. Sitting on the Riviera or
in the Bahamas, sipping cocktails, month after
month with men who only wanted her beauty
and body was not *her*. Yeah, her mum's American hadn't lasted more than a year.

Kristina could love Chase for his sensitivity
alone. But she wouldn't. Loving him for anything would only bring pain. At the end of the
day he was still a man who didn't settle anywhere
for long, didn't gather people around him, didn't
want the same things she did. Though there was a
real possibility he did want them, but wasn't prepared to risk finding them. He wasn't as straightforward as the man who presented himself as
SARCO. That man was in charge, was friendly
without getting involved. The man standing beside her hurt her deep inside where no one was
allowed to go.

Again, she'd not be finding out why because
to do so meant becoming involved, and as much
as she'd like to be there for him, to make a difference, it would come with a price she couldn't
afford. A broken heart was not on her horizon.
Yes, getting close to Chase would mean love.

Because she already felt twinges of emotion that only had one name whenever she was with him. Twinges only, not full-on, heart-totally-involved love. She remembered the lust that had dominated for weeks. 'I'm turning in. See you in the morning unless I'm required for an emergency.'

The haunting sound of a flute wafted over the air. She hesitated, listening as the sweet sound rose and fell. It was coming from the other end of the ship, striking her so that she didn't move in case it stopped.

'Kristina.' Chase's hand covered hers, his fingers slipping between hers. 'Stay with me for a moment.'

'It's beautiful,' she whispered, and slowly leaned back against him. Breathing deeply and slowly, she let the tension ease from her body while absorbing his warmth. A warmth unlike the heat from the sun that had finally dipped beyond the horizon. This was a warmth that filled her with longing and love and hope.

'It is.'

The notes rose and fell as though following the air. Who was playing the instrument? One of the medical people? Or a refugee? They never brought much with them but a flute would take up no space in a small bag.

Chase wound his arms around her, tucked her closer to his body, his chest a wall for her back.

His chin rested on the top of her head, his breaths lifting strands of her hair from behind her ear.

The music soared, and her heart rate followed the tempo.

Chase's hands spread over her waist, held her tightly yet gently.

She didn't want anything to move, could stay like this for hours.

Silence. Disappointment dripped off her. 'Oh,' she whispered. 'That was lovely.'

Then another note hung in the air, followed by more, a faster tempo, one that had her toes tapping.

Chase's hands were turning her, bringing her to face him. 'Let's dance.' He reached for her hands, drew her close as he stepped in time to the tune.

She went with him, unable to refuse, following his lead, hearing the music, hearing the beat in her veins, in her head.

When the music slowed, Chase slowed, held her close, and moved on the spot.

When the notes fell away, Kristina held her breath, waiting for the next tune.

Silence. This time it remained.

But Chase's hands were still holding her, his face coming closer to hers, and then his lips were touching her mouth, a light brush that woke her fully yet left her languid as his mouth covered hers and pressed harder, capturing her, teasing, sending waves of desire to her toes. To her fingers, her belly, her centre.

Winding her arms around his shoulders, she hung on and kissed him back with all the pent-up frustration of the last weeks. She kissed him deeply, hungrily. Kissed him as though to imprint herself on his mind for ever.

'Kristina,' he groaned against her mouth.

She didn't answer. Couldn't for the longing in her throat.

Then she was being gently put aside. 'We have to stop.'

She didn't recognise his throaty voice filled with tension and need. Chase wanted her as badly as she wanted him. So why not do something about it? But as she opened her mouth to say so, she hesitated. He was right. They had to stop. Taking this any further would only exacerbate the differences between them. It would be a short-term thing, and knowing that would hover over her, make her feel uneasy instead of happy. She was too far gone over Chase to be able to have a fling and walk away in one piece. The pendulum was moving, from one side, lust, to the other, love, and she had to stop it going any further.

But couldn't she have one time with him?

He shook his head slowly, apparently good at mind-reading.

Stepping back, Kristina let her hands drop slowly to her sides. 'See you in the morning.'

His hand caught one of hers. 'Goodnight, Kristina.' His thumb caressed her skin, winding up the need tighter than ever. Then he let her go.

Loud banging on their cabin door had Kristina and Jane out of bed and pulling on clothes before hurrying on deck, where people from Libya were being brought on board after a small boat had capsized nearer the coast.

The scene was organised chaos. Small, bedraggled children sat crying and shaking in sodden clothes while distraught adults held them tight, their own tears tracking down ashen faces.

Across the deck Chase was doing CPR on a youngster, the strain in his face saying there was no way he would fail to revive the lad.

She rushed to join him. 'Want a hand?'

'Get the defibrillator,' he demanded, sweat streaming down his cheeks and forehead.

Snatching the machine off the bulkhead, Kristina dropped down beside Chase, placing patches on the boy's chest to attach the wires. 'Stand back.'

The limp body jerked off the deck, slumped back down.

'Again,' demanded Chase. 'Again.'

When the flat line started to rise Kristina's

hopes lifted. 'That's the boy. Where's the oxygen?' she asked.

'Coming,' Chase informed her through gritted teeth. 'Someone else needed it first.'

There was more than one tank and fittings, but when she looked around the deck she could see them all in use. 'What happened?'

'The boat was so overcrowded that when a wave from a passing ship hit, it rolled and sank. Luckily the other ship stopped and tried to save everyone, but it seems some haven't been found.' Chase's face was grim. 'But I've got this one.' He reached for the boy's wrist and felt for his pulse. 'Too weak.'

The boy's eyes flickered open. Water spewed from his lungs.

Chase quickly rolled him onto his side to prevent choking. 'I thought we'd got all that. Seems he's taken in more water than the Mediterranean holds. How did he survive that?'

'Here we go.' Kristina took the gear a nurse was handing her and placed a mask over the boy's face, turning on the valve.

'Hello. My name is Kristina. This is Dr Chase. You are safe now.' Hopefully her tone would do what her words couldn't and give the lad a sense of calm.

'Chase, over here,' called someone. 'We've got a major trauma.'

'You all right here?' he asked, but didn't wait for an answer, loping off across the deck like a wild dog was after him.

'I need a doctor when someone's free.'

Hearing Jane's voice, Kristina looked around. 'What's up?'

'Probably a fractured arm and torn ligaments.'

'Swap. This lad had heart failure, probable cause drowning. His lungs have been cleared, and he's breathing with aid from the tank. Can you watch him?'

'Be right there.'

Kristina counted the beats in her patient's wrist. Light, but regular. Was he really going to be that lucky? Her fingers crossed for him, she wiped his face and mouth.

Jane knelt down on the opposite side. 'Hi, there. I'm Jane. What have you been doing to yourself?'

Kristina headed for the girl with the fracture. 'Hello. I'm a doctor. Kristina is my name.' Her fingers felt the upper right arm that lay at an odd angle. 'I need to get you with one of the surgeons to put you back together.'

'I'll help you carry her down.' A nurse placed a stretcher on the deck beside them.

'Thank goodness for lifts.' Kristina nodded at him. Too much heavy lifting and carrying didn't do her back a lot of good.

'Kristina, over here,' Chase called. 'Now.'

'I'll get someone else to help me with this,' Bernie told her.

'What's up?' She squatted beside Chase, who looked fierce with determination.

'Blunt force trauma to the skull. He's not responding to stimulus, BP's way too low. I'm going into Theatre immediately and need you on hand while we take him down. We can't wait for a chopper to airlift him to the mainland. He won't survive that long. Watch his vitals while I scrub up,' Chase added in no uncertain terms.

'Onto it.' This was like the day the bomb had blown up on the training exercise. With everyone in shock and frantic to do the right thing by the wounded, it had been chaotic. And she hadn't been able to move, to help. A chill settled over her. As long as the outcome was a hundred percent better. So far the chaos did appear to be under control, with everyone getting on with their jobs, all efficiency. She needed to relax. No one was dying from an uncontrollable bleed out. But she couldn't shake the sense of déjà vu, of not doing enough for the wounded. Which made no sense. Tonight she was not incapacitated with injuries and unable to help those who needed her.

As soon as Chase, his patient and a full tally of staff were at the operating table Kristina went looking for someone else to help.

'Over here.' Calvin waved at her.

'What's this one?'

'I suspect a miscarriage. There's heavy bleeding between her thighs and intermittent tightening of the gut at regular intervals. She's hypothermic, hence the survival blanket. We've stripped her of her wet clothes.' Calvin rubbed his chin with the back of a glove-covered hand. 'She's not responding to anything I say. Not a blink or a tightening of her hands. I wonder if it's because I'm a male.'

Kristina reached inside the blanket for a cold hand, and held it gently. 'Hello, can you hear me?' Where was Zala when she needed her? She'd disembarked along with everyone who'd come on board with her weeks ago, and Kristina still thought about her. If only they'd been able to keep her with them, but that was selfish as the girl was getting on with finding her new life. 'My name is Kristina and I'm a doctor.' The words were starting to taste bland after so many times repeating them and not being understood.

The woman was shivering non-stop and her skin was frozen while there was a heatwave going on.

'Let's get her inside,' Calvin suggested. 'Away from the crowds she might be more receptive to help.'

'If that's possible. She's slipping in and out of

consciousness.' Standing, she looked around for another stretcher.

In the full glare of the lights it was apparent Calvin's assessment was correct. The miscarriage was nearly complete, with the afterbirth coming away as Kristina began a thorough examination.

Calvin had put on a face mask. 'That way she might not see my masculine side and go all crazy. Though she's more settled since you joined us.'

'Seems pregnant women are my forté at the moment, despite having a midwife on board.'

'It's that soft, coaxing manner of speaking you have that gets them every time.' He grinned. 'I need to practise more.'

'I can see that working.' Kristina laughed. 'To be on the safe side, I'm doing a D and C.'

Calvin nodded. 'Onto it.'

'No problem.' They'd close the area off and scrub up after cleaning the woman down. 'You're helping me?'

'That's what I meant by *we*.' Again he grinned. 'Unless you want to do it alone.'

'Not at all.' They worked well together, and the woman was soon in a bed, tucked under a blanket with a nurse to watch over her until she woke.

'Back topside, I guess.' Kristina aimed for the stairs.

Chase was ahead, striding out hard and fast.

'Chase,' she called.

He didn't turn or slow.

'Chase, wait for me.'

His legs ate up the distance, his hands fisted at his sides.

Why was he ignoring her? Or was he in a hurry to get to another urgent case? He should still be with the brain trauma patient. Uh-oh. She hesitated. Hadn't the patient made it? His injuries had been extreme, and they'd wondered if he'd been hit by the boat while in the water. Chase would be gutted if he hadn't saved the man. They all felt the loss of a patient but Chase seemed to feel it hardest. It was as though he was on a mission to save everyone who came under his care.

All doctors wanted that outcome, but with Chase she'd seen him go into despair when he'd lost a young girl even when the odds had not been on his side. Despair to the point of being over the top. Why? Was that just his nature? Or had he lost a patient he shouldn't have? Most doctors had failures on their conscience, but to the extent Chase seemed to go? No, there was more to this than he would ever let on.

Something terrible lay in both their pasts, something they'd both suffered, and still did, if Chase's reaction tonight was an indicator. He wouldn't tell her about it, she knew that. Didn't mean she couldn't offer her support. As soon as

they were finished up he'd head for his—their—
space, and she'd be right there for him.

Out on the deck there were few minor injuries
left to deal with, and the nurses were handing out
hot tea and bread with butter.

'We're done,' said Jane when Kristina came to
a halt beside her. 'We're arranging bedding and
dry clothes for those who need it and then we
can stand down.'

'Sounds good to me. It's been quite a night.'
From kissing Chase to fixing the wounded. Her
gaze travelled the length of the deck and found
Chase. He stood talking to one of the new nurses,
his stance tight and unforgiving, his voice low
and controlled, yet anger was coming off him in
waves. Anger at the nurse? Or because of whatever had gone on during the operation?

Jane turned her head to stare in the same direction. 'The head injury guy died on the table.'

'I wondered.' Kristina's heart went out to the
young man's family. And to Chase. He'd be chas-
tising himself for days to come.

'Want a mug of tea?' Jane asked, now watching her.

'Best offer I've had all night.' What would
Chase say if she took him one? Only one way
to find out.

But it wasn't going to happen. He went past
without acknowledging her, yet she'd swear he'd

seen her as he'd stormed away to head down to the cabins, not up to his space. He'd have a lot to see to before knocking off for what remained of the night. Then he did an abrupt about-turn and charged up on deck.

She could give him some time to collect himself. Or she could join him. 'Make that a tea and a coffee,' she told Jane as she watched Chase charge over to the stairs heading to the deck.

Did she go to him or let him be alone and unhappy? That had been raw pain darkening those eyes to thunder clouds. She didn't let friends down when they needed someone to talk to. Not that she had friends who came calling in hours of need, neither was Chase likely to talk to her. But, 'One tea and one coffee,' she repeated.

'Sorry it's not laced with brandy.' Kristina handed Chase a mug when she finally made it to their space a few minutes later.

'Right.'

At least he accepted the proffered coffee. Settling against the railing, she sipped her tea and stared out into the darkness. 'Rough night.'

She was met with silence. Not that she'd been expecting Chase to burst into conversation. But nothing? Yes, that was the man she'd come here to lend a shoulder to. She sipped more tea. 'It never gets any easier, does it?'

Nothing.

'We can't save them all all of the time, Chase.'

Coffee splashed over the deck as the mug jerked in his fingers. 'Yes, I can,' he roared. 'I have to.'

Kristina held still, watched the play of emotions warring in his face and eyes—pain, anger, frustration, need—and knew she'd gone too far. But she wasn't about to back off. He needed help. Not that she was any expert about this kind of pain, only knew from her own experiences how it could destroy a person. 'You're wrong. I've been there. I know.'

'Go, Kristina. Just go.'

So much for that kiss.

CHAPTER FOUR

HE MIGHT'VE KNOWN.

Kristina didn't budge, looked as if she'd stay all night if he didn't respond, if he didn't beg her to leave him alone with his pain. Did she think that because he'd kissed her she had the right to encroach? Chase wanted to slam his fist into a bulkhead, throw a tantrum, yell at her for caring enough to be there. People weren't allowed to care about him—he'd made a career out of pushing away anyone who tried. Not that he'd succeeded with his family. They ignored his outbursts, his cold shoulder, the physical distances he'd put between them ever since that night. They loved him, no question.

Was Kristina made of the same stern stuff? Did he want her to be? It would only lead to heartache—for them both. He was beginning to feel involved with her. To feel the possibility of a future. That kiss had only increased his desire for her, complicating matters further. He had to be strong and push her away.

Chase remained upright with his back against the bulkhead, his hands jammed into the pockets of his shorts and his chin jutting out like an arrow aimed at the distant, unseen horizon. Trying to pretend Kristina wasn't within reach was a joke. Lift an arm and his hand would be touching that creamy skin that managed to survive the worst the sun sent her way without any blemishes. What he wouldn't do to touch, to taste, to kiss that sensational body. To take and to give, another kiss. To lose himself in her. Anything except surrender his heart.

'Chase? Talk to me.'

Why couldn't she leave him in peace? This was *his* place, not *theirs*. Though he had begun thinking of it as theirs. But right now he had to be alone to grapple with the bitterness of another failure. No one died on his watch. No one. Not any more.

But tonight a young man had. The odds of saving him had been long, too long as it turned out. But he should've succeeded. Even when he wasn't a neurosurgeon, and didn't have one on hand. Someone would be bereft, a mother, father, perhaps a wife. Because he'd failed. As he had with Nick.

'There's nothing to talk about,' he howled around the pain of his best friend lying trapped under an immovable beam, dying, pain that mixed with the loss of tonight's patient. 'Go away,' he shouted. Was it his memories he was hollering at? Or Kristina? Either, or: it didn't matter. It was imperative he turn her away before she saw through him to the guilt and fear that ruled him. It wasn't a lie to say there was nothing to talk about. It was called self-protection. Those wounds were not for opening.

They weren't open now?

'We work to save everyone, but it doesn't always pan out like that.' Kristina spoke softly, not daunted by his yelling.

'It has to,' he snapped. What didn't this woman understand? It was straightforward enough. Injured people came to doctors, to *him*, to be fixed, put back together, given another chance at living. 'It's what I trained for.'

'You're right, but sometimes it just isn't enough.' Did she take no umbrage with anything he said? 'Why can't you accept that?'

Get out. Stay. Suddenly he didn't want to push too far. Having Kristina on his side was like a balm he couldn't stop rubbing. Underneath that calm, friendly exterior was a will of steel. One he'd like to get to know. Damn it. Yes, he would. Around Kristina he didn't understand himself any more. It was as though by talking to Ethan so much lately he was allowing himself to dream. Hope rose when she came near. Was it possible to have a future with her? One where he planted his feet in the soil of his own property and felt like he belonged, like he had the right to stay and be happy with Kristina at his side? Deep breaths quietened his racing heart a little. Until he told her, 'Failure doesn't exist in my vocabulary.'

'Everyone knows that. It's the why I'm asking about.'

'Because the consequences are always unbearable for someone. A family, friends.' For me.

She waited. Not a movement, not a smile or a widening of those beautiful eyes. Nothing to get his back up. Nothing to make him believe she felt sorry for him. She was good.

Chase fell into the offer she was making.

'My best friend died. I couldn't save him. I blame myself regardless of the circumstances.'

Still Kristina remained quiet. No ranting about how that was silly, like so many had said to him in the past. Not Reid. He'd also lived with the consequences. Chase shuddered. Something he was accountable for.

'The national junior ski team was competing in the French Alps when an avalanche hit our chalet.'

Now Kristina did move, slipping beside him, her arm touching the length of his. Her warm hand wrapped around his cold one. Then she waited.

'I couldn't help him. Couldn't lift the beam that broke his chest and held him in snow and ice until he was frozen.' The memory of that ice and cold rippled through Chase, lifting his skin, turning his muscles taut.

Kristina's grip tightened. 'You were in the British national team? You must've been extremely skilful.'

'I was.' For all the good it did him or any of the team that night. 'But not the best. Nick Hariday held that ranking, and we were always after him to take over his position. Especially me and Ethan.'

'So that's where Ethan comes into it.' Kristina's nodded. 'Of course.'

'Of course what?' She intrigued him with her easy acceptance of his story. Had she read him correctly? He hoped so, or it was going to sting when he learned differently.

'The initial disquiet between the two of you during those first weeks he was on board. There was such tension between you. At first you both trod on eggshells whenever you were in the same room, but then something changed. You talked, didn't you? About what happened?' She shook her head.

Like he'd said, she was good. Where did that take him? Did he tie her to his side and never let her go so he'd always have someone who understood him to talk to? Or did he shove her away because he'd only drag her down as he hauled her all over the world, searching for more people to save? The one thing he was certain of about Kristina was that she wanted to settle, to stop wandering.

He answered her question in the vague hope it would turn her away. 'There were more beams on top of the one that pinned Nick down. He never stood a chance, but that didn't stop me trying, pleading with him to live. When the futility of my actions finally sank in I turned away to help Ethan. I had to save someone. But I resented him for that.' The words spewed out like poison and he let them come before the lump building in the back of his throat cut off all speech.

This was the second time in weeks that he'd talked about that tragedy. Ethan had brought it up one night on shore during their first three-day break. They'd been downing bourbon, pecking around the past until Ethan had gone for the problem, boots and all, shocking Chase even though he'd known it had to happen. Ethan had put it out there about his guilt at being the one Chase had chosen to save thereby leaving Nick alone in those last precious moments.

For the first time ever Chase had admitted he'd been wrong to let him continue thinking that, how at the time he hadn't known how to cope

with his loss and pain. Still didn't. After that
they'd talked about the guys who hadn't made it,
and the coach who hadn't had the courage to help
anyone and who was now working for a charity
gardening centre, possibly trying to assuage his
conscience. It seemed every survivor from the
tragedy had come away laden with guilt.

The resulting hangover had been a killer. Not
something Chase was about to repeat, even if
there was booze to be had on board, which as far
as he knew there wasn't. It was MFA's policy, and
anyone caught flouting it was politely asked to
leave. Yet tonight, if there had been a bottle on
hand, he might have been sorely tempted, needing the release that came with losing himself in
the hit of alcohol. Not that he made a habit of
doing that but occasionally it was okay.

Unable to resist her any longer, he drew Kristina close and wound his arms around that warm
body, his chin resting on her head as he breathed
in the salt air and her scent. As he waited for the
lump to dissolve and his heart rate to return to
normal, he absorbed her warmth, marvelled at the
wonder of having a woman relax in his embrace,
of not demanding anything for herself, letting
him talk as he wanted to, or not if he preferred.

The lump of pain and despair slowly dissolved
while the throb of his heart began picking up
its beat. His nerve endings came alive one at a

time. His hands splayed on her waist. His mouth hungered for one more kiss. The rest of his body wanted everything, the whole naked, close, orgasmic thing. Tipping back in her arms, he gazed down into her eyes and asked, "Kristina?"

She must've felt the tightening in his body and known his need because she rose onto her toes and leaned forward. 'Yes.' Her husky voice brushed his skin, heightened his yearning. 'Yes.'

As her mouth opened under his he sank further into her embrace. She tasted sweet and strong and dangerous. He wanted to rob her of all awareness except for him. To take her where he was headed. To oblivion. Away from all that screwed him inside out.

There was no noise; no people talking or arguing, no birds squawking overhead, no boats heading towards the ship. Chase was deaf. And hot. And cold. And warm. He was lost in this woman who seemed to understand him when she shouldn't. She stole his ability to think, gave of herself and endorsed his feeling of being in the right place at the right time with the right woman.

His lips cruised over hers, devoured her mouth as he tasted. Her hands pushed under his shirt to caress and sensitise his skin, and he fell further into her. Rapid breathing made her breasts rise and fall against his chest, inflaming him more.

He had to taste them. Her hips pressed against his rising, hardening need. Her scent swirled around them, enticing, erotic. His hands sought and found hot, bare skin, felt the frantic throb of a pulse, knew the warmth and care being given to him.

'Chase.' An urgent whisper against his mouth cut through the haze.

'What?' He wasn't stopping for anyone. He couldn't. Didn't have the brakes to haul on.

'Chase.' This time his name sounded urgent, and there was a cooling against his chest as the heat source pulled back. 'We've got company.'

His eyes ripped open. His hands dropped to his sides as he stepped back abruptly, the air suddenly chilly 'Who?' Damn it. Why couldn't he have one night to himself? With Kristina and no one to interrupt? *Because you're in charge of what happens on board this vessel where patients and medical staff are concerned.*

'Sorry, Chase, but we've got a problem below deck. One of the men is trying to steal food from the kitchen and the cook's going ballistic.' Calvin's words brought Chase back to reality faster than anything else could.

What had he been doing? About to do? Putting Kristina aside, he ran his hands over his face and straightened his back. 'On my way.'

* * *

'And that's that. He could've said something before rushing away. One word would've done.' Kristina stared after Chase as he bounded along the deck. 'Good to know where I stand.' Like a sticking plaster for his wounds that could be torn off at any moment.

Except the wound was a long way off healing. She wasn't so naïve as to believe she'd helped him on the first step towards forgiving himself. Only he could do that, and *if* there was anyone able to help him it was Ethan, not her.

Her fingers traced the outline of her swollen lips. Hell, could the man kiss. He'd exploded through her, taking away all sense of time, sound, location. All she'd known was Chase—and wanting more, wanting it all. His mouth, those large, strong hands doing a number on her skin, his erection hard against her soft stomach weren't enough. They'd been in a bubble. Until Calvin had turned up, spoiling the moment, bringing her back to reality in a flash. How she'd heard him calling Chase was beyond her.

If only he hadn't. Then who knew where she and Chase might've ended up? Or what they might've done? She should be thankful they'd been interrupted then, and not five minutes later. But she wasn't. She wanted him. Big time. Not sex. *Lovemaking.* She shivered. Yeah, she'd gone and lost sight of what she should be hanging onto and was starting to fall under his spell.

As for what Chase thought? Who knew? He'd rushed away without a backward glance, putting her in her place quick smart.

Chase had been through a lot. She understood his need to be in control, and wanting to save everyone who came his way. But he had to learn not to beat himself up when he lost a patient. As she'd begun accepting she couldn't have saved Corporal Higgs the day the owner of Merrywood's electrical business had been electrocuted while putting in wires at the garage she'd happened to be going past and she had made amends for failing Higgs by saving George.

Unfortunately, it wouldn't be her showing Chase how to move on. They might have shared kisses beyond her wildest imagination, their bodies might be hollering for each other, but they weren't *going* anywhere together. They had too many hang-ups to be able to have even a half-normal relationship. But she'd happily go for more here in their space. Though now she was coming down to earth she knew they wouldn't be making love here. Too risky that they'd be caught. Some people would say that was half the fun. Not her.

It was time to get some shut-eye. The horizon was lightening, and soon the ship would be alive with more people requiring attention. Another boat had been sighted and was due to be intercepted to remove the refugees later in the morning and she needed to be on her A game.

As if she'd get any sleep with those kisses so vivid in her mind. With how her body had reacted to Chase's touches.

She knuckled her back as she slouched along to her cabin. *Please let me sleep,* was her last thought for the night.

'Kristina, wake up. You're needed in the medical room.' Jane was shaking her arm.

Kristina rolled onto her back and stared at the apparition above her. 'What time is it?'

'You've missed breakfast.' Jane grinned. 'I'm not going to ask who kept you up so late.'

'Get a life,' she muttered. 'I was busy.'

'Sure you were. If it's any consolation, Chase looks terrible, too.'

'You're saying I look bad? How?' There was a low pounding going on in her skull, but how could she *look* a mess? They'd only kissed. *Only* kissed? Those kisses had been right up there with X-rated warnings. Her skin was probably scorched.

'Yuk, now you're looking dreamy. Definitely time you were downing strong coffee and dealing with malarial fevers.' Jane headed for the cabin door. 'If I don't see you in ten, I'll be back to prod you awake again.'

Kristina swung her legs out of the bunk and sat up to drop her head into her hands. Her eyes drooped shut. She forced them open. 'I'll be there. Give me five for a shower, and pour the strongest coffee that machine's capable of.'

'Will do.' Jane disappeared, closing the door behind her with a snap.

Hauling herself upright, Kristina's head floated and her body ached. If this was the result of Chase's kisses she was better off without them. Or had it been the reruns in her dreams that had wiped her out? Whichever, she didn't need any more.

Try telling that to someone who believes you. Imagine what making love with Chase would be like. Her imagination had already done that, now she was ready for the real thing.

The cold shower went some way to clearing the fog from her brain, and the coffee dispelled the rest, leaving her mind clear to focus on what was important around here—patients. 'That was perfect, Jane.'

'You're welcome.' Her cabin mate winked. 'Come and meet your next patient. He came on board yesterday, didn't complain of any ailments, yet during the night his temperature rose to thirty-eight point five and he developed sweats, chills and abdo pain. I'm thinking malaria so I've taken an EDTA blood and made a film. I'll stain it when it's dry.'

The thin, sweating man curled up on the mattress had a faint yellow tinge to his skin, suggesting his liver was reacting to whatever was causing the other symptoms. Kristina nodded. 'You're right. It looks like a case of malaria.' She'd seen a few since joining the ship. 'We need to determine which type but I'll give him a dose of chloroquine phosphate in the meantime.' It was the drug of choice for all but the rarest form of malaria and no harm would be done by administering it.

'I'll keep wiping him down and trying to get fluids into him. Shall we go for intravenous fluids as well?'

'Definitely. Dehydration needs to be kept at bay.' Kristina went to the drug cabinet and put in the code to activate the lock. Retrieving the chloroquine phosphate, she signalled Jane to check the vial and date, then returned to kneel beside the man. 'I'm giving you an injection,' she said, even though she wasn't sure he could hear her, and wouldn't understand her.

'Thank you.' His eyes flicked open, closed again.

He understood English. Yay. 'Have you had malaria before?'

'Yes.'

'Do you know what type?'

'Ovale?' Again he opened his eyes. 'Not sure.'

'Plasmodium ovale. I'll look at your blood film as soon as it's ready.' Sometimes a blood slide showed many parasites in the red cells, but more often they were difficult to find with less than one per field of a hundred or more red cells. This was work for a lab technician, and there wasn't one available. Chase had studied blood films and haematology so that he could diagnose some of the diseases their patients came with. She knew enough to recognise a parasite in the red cells when she saw one down the microscope and could run them by him for confirmation.

'I'm Kristina, a doctor. What's your name?' She pressed the plunger on the syringe she'd inserted into his arm.

'Abdal Matin.' A sheen of sweat covered his face. 'I worked in England five years ago as a reporter.'

How had he ended up here? It wasn't something she felt she could ask. 'Have you been taking prophylaxis?'

His mouth flattened and anger appeared in his unsteady gaze. 'I took chloroquine until it became impossible to get.'

Even when she had no idea where he'd come from or been, it was on record how difficult getting medical care had become in the places these people came from. 'Jane's going to set you up for intravenous fluids, and I want you to try and drink as much water as possible. You have a high temperature and those sweats aren't helping your fluid levels.'

'Thank you.'

Kristina got herself a top-up of coffee to take through to the tiny cabin where the microscope and glass containers of stain waited. A purple-coloured blood film lay on a blotter, ready to be looked at.

Perching on a stool, she applied a drop of oil to the slide and slid it in place on the microscope. Leaning forward, she focused the lens and began scanning the film, noting higher numbers of white cells than normal, mainly neutrophils and band forms, confirming the infection her patient had. The platelet numbers appeared normal. The red cells showed no obvious abnormalities but, then, she was no haematology expert. What was important was finding malarial parasites and they weren't exactly waving flags.

Thirty minutes later Kristina stood up to stretch her leg muscles and rub her lower back where the familiar throbbing had started up.

'Nothing?' Chase asked from the doorway.

She let her hand fall away. 'There's still a lot of film to go over.' Glancing over at him, her breath stuck in her throat. At the moment that mouth mightn't be soft but she had the memories, and they were turning her stomach into a swirling mess of need.

'You had breakfast?'

'I'm not hungry.'

His head tilted to one side. 'I could remind you what you said to me the other day on that subject.'

'I need to keep looking for malaria.' Her stomach would reject any food she fed it.

'You can eat and study the slide at the same time.' That wonderful mouth slipped into a smile, aimed directly at her.

And finished off any last hope of eating. 'I'll grab something when I've finished here. The man speaks English, by the way, so we currently have another interpreter, or will when the fever's abated.'

'What nationality is he?'

'I have no idea.'

'Let's hope it's the right one to be of use over the coming days.' The smile widened, lifting the corners of those delicious lips further.

What she wouldn't do for another kiss. 'At the moment he's too ill to be worrying about helping us out.'

Chase stepped into the small cabin, tall and lean and sexy as hell, making her want to throw herself at him. 'Kristina.' He spoke softly. 'About last night…'

'Kristina, your malaria man is asking for you.' Jane stood where Chase had been moments before.

'Right, thanks.' Her eyes were still focused on Chase.

'We'll talk later.' His smile hadn't faded so he couldn't have been going to say something she didn't want to hear, like 'Sorry for kissing you' or 'That was wrong' or 'Forget the things I told you'. Could he?

That would hurt, she realised in a moment of clarity. The few men she'd dated she'd usually left without a backward glance on her part. This was a jaw-dropping shock. Not that there'd been many males in her life, as in affairs or the like, and none had got close enough to touch her in a way that raised hope and awareness for those wishes of a home and family. Was this what it was like to fall in love? It had better not be. Chase was all wrong for her. Given her history of mucking up her big goals, like joining the army to find a 'family', there was every possibility she'd get this thing with Chase wrong, too. Her parents had not shown her how to get it right.

'Sure.' Stepping around him, making sure not to brush against that delicious body in case he thought she was making a play for him, she headed for the door. 'I'll see Abdal Matin and then grab a sandwich.'

'I've got a few minutes going spare. I'll take a look at the slide.'

'Go for it.' If he found a parasite she'd try not to be disappointed she hadn't discovered it.

'Get out of here. You're needed in the medical area.' There might be a smile beaming out at her but she still felt let down.

She'd been hoping Chase wanted her—in a totally different way from how a patient might. At least he was still smiling. That was unusual in itself.

She'd take what she could get. *Pitiful, Kristina. Really, really pathetic. You're almost begging for his attention.*

'Plasmodium ovale,' Chase informed her when she returned to where he was.

'You found it? Damn, I wanted to do that.'

He shrugged a shoulder. 'That's the knocks you get in this work. Come and have a look.' He pushed the stool back enough for her stand in front of the microscope and study the cells at the other end of the lens. 'The ring form could be any type, but that parasite in the centre of the field? Definitely ovale.'

The purple, blue and red shades of the circle and dots were strong. 'It's incredible how something unable to be seen by the naked eye can cause so much harm to a human.' She glanced over her shoulder and stopped breathing.

Chase's gaze was fixed on her backside, nothing but longing gleaming out of his eyes.

'Chase?' she squeaked.

His head jerked up. 'Um, what were you saying?'

'Nothing.' Important, she added silently.

'I'll get back to the operating table.' The stool rocked as he leapt to his feet and stepped around her.

'Chase, stop it. You don't have to rush away.'

'Yes, Kristina, I do. For your sake, if not mine.'

Watching him stride out of the room as though he was being chased by a malaria-laden mosquito, she sank onto the stool he'd just vacated. Chase had just told her where they stood. Bluntly and purposefully. His beguiling smile didn't mean they had something going between them, had not meant what she'd begun dreaming about.

You didn't want anything happening with Chase. Other than more kisses. And making love.

All off the menu, by the look on his face as he'd fled the cabin.

Might pay to stay away from Chase's corner on deck tonight. Every night? He could think she was staying away because he was a lost cause. That she couldn't cope with his past. Or he might be relieved because one of them had to see sense and call a halt to this attraction steaming between them.

Tossing her sandwich in the bin, she went to find a patient who needed her undivided attention. Chase could wait. She wasn't done with him, though. Not by a long shot.

CHAPTER FIVE

'I KNOW I should've phoned days ago, but it's bedlam here right now. Anyone would think our quiet little marriage ceremony was competing with the latest British royal wedding. Don't tell people you're getting married until the deed's done,' Claire said breathlessly. 'Honestly, you'd think the whole village had been waiting for ever for me to announce this marriage.'

Kristina laughed away the pain at the idea of her ever having to plan her own wedding. 'Says she who sounds very happy.'

'I am so happy it's scary. And we will have a party at home sometime later, but I won't be wearing a lace train that's twenty metres long or carrying a bouquet that would require a crane to lift. A glass of champagne will be enough, though with junior on board the bubbles will be water, not wine.' Claire paused, then went on in a quieter voice, 'I didn't know people could be so caring. Ethan's having fits about it.'

'I bet he is.' Kristina could imagine him glancing over his shoulder for an escape route. 'But he'll stay. He loves you.'

'I know. I truly believe that.'

Again Kristina had to swallow hard. She was happy for this woman who'd befriended her on the ship. 'I'm glad for you both.'

'I rang to say you're going to be my bridesmaid. I won't take no for an answer.'

'But you haven't known me very long. You must have other friends for this.'

'No, it's you I want, and shall have. We clicked from the beginning, and that's what matters. Not even the fact that Chase is standing by Ethan on the day will let you out of this.'

He hadn't mentioned it. Was he unhappy about having to stand by her, all dressed up? Come on, they'd kissed and were still on speaking terms. There'd even been a second round of kisses. A frisson of excitement ran through her. Even small weddings had a photographer, didn't they? She'd keep one of those photos of her and Chase in her drawer to take out on the rainy days. 'Thank you. I can't wait.'

'Thanks, Kristina. It means a lot to me.'

'You asking means a lot.' Gulp. *Don't do the sentimental stuff. It gets messy.* 'What am I to do about a dress? Have you got ideas on style and colour?'

'Soft blue and off the shoulder. Anything else

is your choice. Don't forget shoes with heels to die for. Make the men salivate.'

'I don't need men drooling over me.' Kristina laughed. Her feet were still more used to heavy-duty boots than killer heels. It really was time to get a girlie life. This could be fun.

'Might make Chase take notice in ways he mightn't have yet.' When Kristina gasped, Claire continued, 'Has he already? Come on. How *is* it going between the two of you?'

'You'd better have a stand-in ready in case I decide not to turn up for your wedding.'

Claire just laughed. 'Touched a nerve, did I?'

It was fun talking like this, even if her friend ignored the boundaries. It could be time to let go of more of her hang-ups. 'We're getting on better than expected.' *Oh, please.* 'We meet every night at Chase's no-go zone on deck.'

'Chase letting you be there says heaps.'

'There have been one or two interesting conversations.' Not to mention those kisses.

Claire went to the heart of the matter. 'What aren't you telling me?'

'That I like Chase a lot, really like him. But I doubt we'll take it very far as he's not into long-term relationships and, to be fair, he's made sure I understand that.'

'Ethan wasn't into them either until I came along and changed his mind.'

'I am not getting—' *Stop. Claire will be upset if you finish that sentence.* It wasn't as though she'd deliberately got pregnant, but she might misconstrue what Kristina had been about to say. 'Chase has told me a little of what happened when their ski team was hit by the avalanche. He has some huge issues to work through. The way I see it, he's not trying to move forward, instead seems focused on the past and how to rectify the impossible.'

Chase had told her that in confidence, but she needed to air her concerns, and to whom better than Claire, who already knew what drove their men? Their men? Chase wasn't hers. Yet there was something between them that went further than she'd ever experienced. Resisting him would be nigh on impossible—if they were ever to get hot and bothered together again.

'I shudder every time I think about that avalanche,' Claire agreed. 'I know the guys are still dealing with what happened and how they sort of hated each other, and are now becoming firm friends, but don't let Chase hold that up as a reason not to get involved if you're beginning to feel something for him.'

The many times Chase dominated her mind, not to mention her body, had not distracted her enough to put plans on hold for finding somewhere to settle and get a job. There was only one person looking out for her on that score, and that was her. 'You'd make a great agony aunt,' she joked, while the weight of what she might be losing out on dragged at her heart.

'Any time you have questions, you have my number. But, seriously, be open-minded about this. I'm speaking from experience here.'

'Thanks, Claire.' Swallow. Friendship. Wow. 'I've got to go. There's a boatload of refugees coming on board. We'll talk more about the wedding soon.' Without waiting for an answer, Kristina ended the call and slipped the phone into her pocket. Claire was too easy to talk to. Like Chase.

Looking around the deck, her gaze instantly found him. Standing with a nurse and a young man holding his meagre possessions in a ragged pack, Chase looked alone as he issued details of medical requirements. Tall, imposing and in control of all that was around him, there was no doubting his ability to oversee the comings and goings of the ship and its occupants. He was achieving what he desperately wanted, yet there was something sad about his stance. It spoke of disconnection, of deliberate composure to keep everyone at bay, of not letting anyone see the real Chase Barrington.

She was beginning to see behind that mask to the longing and fear, even the love he was capable of if only he'd risk himself. Strange how he allowed her into his corner. Only once had he told her to go away, and she'd chosen to ignore him, and look where that had led. Revelations followed by electric kisses, almost followed by making love.

Most times he seemed pleased when she turned up. Sometimes she thought he was almost relieved, as if needing reassurance she wouldn't let him down. Since he wasn't into relationships it didn't add up. Could be she read too much into what for him was simply a friendship. A friendship with hot kisses and nearly sex? No, they'd moved beyond being pals. What came next was anyone's guess.

Chase turned, his eyes meeting hers. Then his mouth lifted into a soft smile that warmed her to her toes. That smile was genuine, and to be treasured. Bit by bit the man behind the caution was coming to light. Their kisses had softened her determination to remain strong against people who could hurt her, and had her wondering if Chase might be the one to eventually tear all her barricades down. Talk about a huge leap of trust that she wasn't ready to chance this side of the next ten Christmases. But she could give him a smile filled with happiness in return.

His eyes widened and his smile deepened. She'd get on with the day in a cheery frame of mind, and stop wondering if Chase was right for her. If he was, then things would unfold at the right time. If he wasn't, they'd move on from each other, maybe cross paths occasionally at events like the wedding. The naming ceremony for Claire and Ethan's baby perhaps. As if it would be that simple.

Claire had found her soul mate. What was that like? Finding a man who'd accept her for who she was and give her the love she craved? She'd have to love him back as strongly, or what would be the point? A rigid relationship like the one Kristina had with her parents wasn't happening. Chase might be aloof but he didn't do cold, much as he tried to pretend differently.

Did she truly believe that? The dreams that romped through her head at night where they were always together—working, playing, living—said so. In those he was always fun, kind and laughing. Which wasn't likely to become real. Dreams were nothing more than uncontrolled hope flitting through her mind when she wasn't in a position to stop them.

Moving away, she vowed to get on to looking into GP vacancies as soon as she had time to herself. It wasn't fair to expect Jarrod to come up with what she required.

'Why aren't there any jobs available where I'd like to live?' Kristina muttered as she shuffled her backside on the hard deck and leaned against the bulkhead, trying to stay out of the sun, still strong as it slid beyond the horizon.

'You being too picky?'

Chase. Where had he come from? How long had he been standing there? Why hadn't her radar warned her? 'Probably.'

'What are you looking for?' He sat down beside her, stretching those long legs for ever, and folding his arms across that expansive chest that stretched his T-shirt over interesting muscles that she itched to touch, to kiss, to lick.

In other words, diverting her attention to places it had no right to go. 'Something permanent.'

'So you've said. Are you sure you want to settle down? No more travelling the world, using your medical skills to help others?'

Did he have to make it sound so dull? So ordinary? It was what she longed for. 'Yes. My skills are just as useful at home, working in a medical centre, as here.'

'Home as in Manchester?'

'I have no wish to return to Manchester.' Now she looked up from the website listing medical positions all over Britain that she'd been scrolling through and focused entirely on her inquisitor. 'I prefer the south of England.'

'A small town like Merrywood.' When she gasped he added, 'It's written all over your face.'

She looked away. 'It can't be.' She'd become an expert at hiding her feelings.

'Was your boarding school in Manchester?'

'Yes, but Dad wasn't most of the time so no weekend catch-ups. Anyway, that's history, doesn't pertain to anything here. My problem is that I'll be unemployed in a little over four weeks, and that makes me nervous. I like to know where I'll be at any point in time. I plan my year to know what I'll be doing and where I'll be doing it, except I only got close to six months sorted this time.' She stared at him, hoping he'd understand her need to find her little spot in the world, a place that didn't require major worries about how to survive while making sure others could, too.

'You just argued with yourself. Your past is driving your future.' Breaking eye contact, his head tapped the bulkhead as he tipped it back and stared out in front of them.

The sea and sky had merged on the horizon so it was impossible to tell where one started and the other finished. 'Sometimes that's how I feel,' Kristina conceded. 'What you said is true for everybody.'

'Why this need to settle down?'

'It's what women in their thirties do.' She glanced at him. 'And, no, the biological clock's not ticking. I've been looking for somewhere to call my own since the day I overheard the girls at boarding school saying I didn't belong in their dorm, that I was dumb.' Following on from her mother not wanting her and her dad dumping her into someone else's care, the girls had only confirmed what she'd learned. She wasn't lovable, or likable.

Chase took her hand in his, clasped them together on his thigh. 'So why the army? Why *Medicine For All*? Why didn't you buy a house in any town and join the local medical practice when you qualified?'

'Shouldn't you be checking on patients? Or organising rosters?' She couldn't find the strength to withdraw her hand. It felt as though it was in the right place. Neither should she continue talking about her past. But there was nothing of interest to divert her attention on the medical jobsite. She closed that down with her free hand.

'The rosters are up to date, all vacancies filled again. The refugees are in capable hands or sleeping.'

Rare indeed for Chase to be letting go that easily. The blue in the sea was darkening to black, whereas in the sky it was as though the colour was slowly draining away to leave behind a star-studded canvas. Relaxing, she gave in to the need to talk.

'A recruitment officer for the armed forces was at a school where I was working on an immunisation programme and we had lunch together at the back of a classroom away from raging teenagers and bored teachers. He talked about the services and how he'd belonged to the army since he'd left school and it felt more like family than his parents and brothers ever had.' That had struck a chord with her. 'He mentioned how everyone in the unit always had his back in a way he'd never known before. I signed up within two months.'

'Was he right?'

'Yes.' She sighed. 'And no. I always knew the men and women around me had my back, wherever we were stationed. I belonged to them, to the greater picture. We ate, drank, worked together twenty-four seven, to the point it got claustrophobic and I'd wish I was out in the real world again. Until I was discharged. Obtusely then I wanted back in.' Much like the day her father had deposited her at that boarding school and told her she had to stand on her own feet and not be so needy. Apparently wanting to be loved by her parents was wrong.

'There were no jobs you could've done if you'd stayed in?'

'Nothing I wanted. The medical side was basic on home base. My back injuries stymied me from ever again being able to carry a twenty-five-kilo pack for hours on end. There were desk jobs, except pen-pushing didn't appeal.'

'It's always the paperwork that rubs me up the wrong way, but there's no avoiding it, I'm afraid. Not that I've found anyway.'

'When you do, copyright the idea. You'll make a fortune.'

'Now, there's a thought. But what would I do with said fortune? I'd want to be philanthropic but it takes time to look into charities and make decisions about who to donate money to. Time that would keep me away from surgeries and medical cases.'

'Which is what keeps you moving.'

Chase's hand jerked around her fingers. 'Yes.'

Kristina left it at that and studied the stars appearing in their thousands.

'There's a shooting star.' Chase pointed to the west.

The glittering light shot across the sky. 'I'm making a wish,' she chuckled. *To finally find what I've been searching for.* Her hand tightened around Chase's.

'Don't tell me what you wish for or it won't come true.'

Not a chance. Some things were best kept secret regardless of the consequences. Now she wanted another star on the move, because suddenly she really, really wanted to wish for Chase to kiss her. She could make the first move but what if he pushed her away? What if he told her the other night couldn't be repeated? Instigating a kiss then being rejected would humiliate and hurt. To hell with it. She'd take the risk.

But as she turned toward Chase he stood up and leaned down to tug her gently. 'Join me up here, will you?'

Then she was in his arms and his mouth was covering hers. No need for another shooting star. Certain dreams came true because they were meant to. Kristina gave up thinking and succumbed to Chase and his mouth, his chest pressing against her breasts and those hands splayed across her back. The hard rod pressing into her stomach. Heat spread slowly throughout her body, warming her in places that had been cold for far too long. This she could get to like permanently.

Her lungs squeezed tight. What?

Chase's mouth left hers. 'Kristina? You all right?'

Permanently? With Chase? It wasn't happening. *Am I all right?* 'Absolutely,' she whispered, before returning her mouth to his, afraid he'd walk away before she'd finished with him. More than all right. As long as she didn't think about that permanent word.

Chase deepened the kiss and she forgot everything except the man delivering this wonder. Forgot common sense, disregarded the warning bells clanging in the back of her head, and went with him to some place she'd never been before. And that was only with a kiss.

'Have you decided what you're doing for your days off?' Jane asked Kristina as the two of them worked on a young girl with a fever related to an infection in a wound in her thigh.

At the next bed Chase palpated a man's belly and held his breath as he listened for Kristina's answer. It was a question he'd been pondering, with an idea he wasn't certain was right brewing in the back of his mind.

Kristina drew up a dose of antibiotics. 'I'm thinking I'll do some sightseeing around Marseille, might even go to Nice for a day or into Italy. The trains run all the time. And I'll soak for hours in the spa at the hotel where MFA has booked our rooms.'

He had his answer. Two days before everyone headed off in different directions and he was already thinking how much he'd miss Kristina. Those times they had to themselves on the deck held him enthralled. 'The idea of the break is to get well away from the ship and the problems it's connected to.' The words spilled out of his mouth. True though they were, he suspected Kristina might be avoiding going back to England for her time off because there was no one she especially wanted to catch up with.

'I won't be on board, I'll be at the hotel. What's everyone else doing?' She was good at redirecting a conversation when it got too close for comfort.

Jane answered, 'I'm heading to Majorca, where my boyfriend's got an apartment. He's flying out from London to be with me. Three days of sun, swimming and lots of sangria. What more could a girl want?'

'It sounds sublime.' Kristina laughed, but there was a hint of sadness in the depths of her eyes.

Chase hated seeing that. He wanted to cheer her up, make her laugh. Stepping away from his patient, he told them, 'I'm going to my mother's sixtieth birthday shindig.'

After hearing about Kristina's sad family life, he'd rethought how lucky he was and had given in to the demands from Libby and his father to turn up for his mother's special occasion. Feeling like the heel he was for avoiding most family gatherings, he'd been mortified at his mother's joy. He really had become a terrible son, and while he believed he was protecting himself from further pain there no denying he'd hurt his family in the process. 'I'll be staying at my parents' farm.'

'Nice.' Kristina wiped the girl's arm and slid the needle in. The girl didn't wince.

'Want to join me?' he asked into a sudden silent moment. It was awkward because whatever her answer everyone would hear it, and know he'd got friendly with her when it was general knowledge he didn't do friendships. Except now he did. Reid had refused to be pushed away, had insisted they had a lot to work on and an underlying respect for each other despite Nick's death hanging between them. Despite, or because of?

During the weeks Ethan had been on board he'd begun to question everything he'd held onto since the tragedy and had realised how much he admired Ethan and always had, that what he'd believed to be strong dislike when they had been teens had actually been envy because the guy had been a better skier than him. None of that made him feel any better about himself.

Kristina's eyes widened and the empty syringe shook in her hand. 'What did you say?'

Here was the chance to backtrack, to reword the invitation. He didn't do inviting women to his parents' home on those rare occasions he visited. His mother and Libby would be asking questions there were no answers to. 'Want to go to Somerset for our down time? You already know half the clan.'

Get that, anyone listening in? Kristina's no

stranger to my family. This is a friendly invitation, not what you might be thinking.

Kristina stared at him as though he'd lost his mind.

He had. He was going to regret it if she answered yes. Though right now disappointment was gathering like storm clouds the longer she remained quiet.

The silence around them grew, as if everyone was waiting for Kristina's answer. When Chase glanced around he saw one or two people watching them but most were engrossed in patients—or pretending to be. Returning his gaze to Kristina, he held his breath.

'Thank you for offering but I'll stay in France.'

His gut dropped. So did his heart. Why? 'Okay, if that's what you want, but in case you change your mind the offer remains until nine tomorrow morning when I leave for the airport.' Relief should be flooding in at her turning him down. Instead he felt piqued. Did he really want Kristina visiting his parents? Libby wasn't known for keeping her mouth shut when it came to her brother; all part of her agenda to make him get over the past and return home to settle. As for his mother, she'd see Kristina as a challenge, a woman to get onside. Still, the disappointment at his offer being declined was growing.

'Thank you.' The syringe rolled between her fingers.

'Careful. You could do yourself some damage with that.' Returning to his patient, he was soon left looking for something else to do. Seeing the doctor rostered to assist him with some minor surgical procedures shortly, he tracked through the waiting refugees. 'Calvin, see you in ten?'

There was a list as long as the table of these procedures to be done but since the cleaners had taken over scrubbing out the area after the last shift knocked off, they weren't able to start earlier.

'Not long now,' Chase told patients as he strode past, hands forced open, a tight smile stretching his face. What was wrong with joining him for a few days' R and R? 'Afterwards there'll be meals waiting for you,' he added when he noticed one of the men repeating everything to the others. Worried smiles broke out. They had yet to learn that when he gave his word it would be kept, and by the time they did they'd gone from the ship and on to whatever awaited them next.

A little after two, Chase and Calvin downed tools and went to grab a bite to eat. 'That was some line-up,' he muttered around his sandwich. He ached from head to toe from standing over the operating table for so long, but at least this in-

take would be ready to leave the ship when they
docked at Marseille. 'You'd think I'd be used to
it.'

'Throw in the late nights we work as well and
the hours stack up really quickly.'

Kristina and Freja wandered into the room,
picked up plates of salad and bread rolls and came
towards them. Both of the girls looked as exhausted as he felt. It was definitely time for that
break.

'We had twin girls this morning,' Freja told
them with a smile. 'So pretty.'

Kristina sat at the furthest end and tore into
her roll hungrily.

'You helped with the birth?' Chase asked, because he wanted to hear her sweet voice.

Her ponytail swung as she shook her head.
'I've been assisting Jorge with vaccinations. Hope
that's all right?'

'Of course it is.' He couldn't remember what
she was rostered on, but he had no problems with
what she'd done.

'I'll get to the children and their check-ups
as soon as I've finished lunch.' Kristina lifted a
water bottle to those wonderful lips and guzzled
half the contents, her eyes closed.

Desire swiped him; hard and sharp. The air
hummed. His lungs didn't know whether to
breathe in or out. It would take one look from

her and he'd be leaping up to sweep her into his arms and race along to his cabin where he'd make love to her, long and deliciously slow—if he had the stamina to hold on for long and slow.

Kristina yawned. 'Sorry.'

Chase collected his scattered brain cells and pulled himself together. This was absolutely silly. Losing control in front of staff in a place where he couldn't do a thing about what was ripping him apart, with a woman who kissed like a she-devil and had then said she wouldn't go home with him was doing his head in—not to mention other parts of his taut body.

Why wouldn't she go to Somerset? Though if this was how he reacted in a dining room where half a dozen medics were eating lunch then he should be grateful. He wouldn't be able to keep his hands to himself as they walked in the fields or sat at the local, having a beer.

Right now he needed to be busy. Very busy. Carefully adjusting his trousers before standing, he took his plate to the dishwasher, trying not to watch Kristina as she sat, chewing slowly, her eyes still half-shut, exhaustion leaking out of her like sauce on an upside-down pudding.

Grabbing a coffee, Chase headed for his office and the pile of paperwork that had come in on the helicopter that morning. Along with the papers there'd been a load of medical supplies they'd run out of due to the unprecedented number of minor surgeries performed over the last three days. At the time he'd have preferred that the satchel had been dropped on the other side of the railing so it could have sunk to the bottom of the sea, but now he was glad of something to occupy his restless mind.

Not that work calmed his rampant hormones. Hopefully getting deeply engrossed in refugee numbers and the amount of flour Pierre needed would eventually settle everything back into place. Until next time Kristina was in his breathing space.

'Chase, got a minute?' Kristina stood in the doorway.

No, his mind roared. 'What's up?' he said aloud. Now, there was a loaded question. He shifted from one foot to the other.

Her tongue wetted her bottom lip. 'Please, don't think I'm being ungrateful, turning down your offer.'

'I don't. But the dogs are going to be disappointed.'

'What?' Her head flicked back so she was staring at him, and then a soft smile lightened the moment, made him fight to stop himself wrapping his arms around her. 'You've got dogs?'

'Not me, my mother. She's bananas about her two German shepherds, and they go crazy around visitors, especially those who take them walking in the fields.'

'Low blow, mister. I love dogs. Once I settle I'm getting one, maybe two.' Her eyes were alight with excitement.

'So you might change your mind about going to the farm—because of dogs, and not me?' He grinned to show no hard feelings, and made a mental note to buy the biggest, juiciest bones in the village if she said yes to going with him.

'You push a hard bargain. But…' Her shoulders rose slowly. 'But I have a dress to buy, and I still need to look into finding a job.'

'You can do that in Somerset as easily as in Marseille.' At least his knees weren't on the floor as he all but begged. 'I know how much you want to resolve the employment problem, but there's nothing wrong with having some fun while you're doing it.'

'You're persistent, aren't you?'

'I've been known to be.' Usually when it was to get something for a patient, not when it came to a beautiful woman he couldn't get out of his head. But he'd never been faced with this dilemma before and was like a blind man trying to follow a track through the forest.

'Jarrod told me to drop by once I'd finished with MFA.'

'Kristina, can you take a look at Abdal Matin

when you've got a moment?' A nurse appeared between them. 'His temperature's spiking again.'

'Coming right now.' She locked thoughtful eyes on him. 'Talk later.'

His heart sank. That meant she was still saying no to his invitation. He had to accept it, or risk looking like a prize prat.

So Jarrod kept in touch with her. He'd sung Kristina's praises when she'd worked for him. Who wouldn't? She'd do anything for her patients, and Chase believed she'd do the same for a partner and any children they might have. Lucky guy, whoever that man might be. Because she would meet someone to love and care about her. How could she not when she was so beautiful, inside and out?

You could be that man.

Using his heel to slam the door shut, he stomped across the narrow space to the desk. He did not want to be that man.

You're sure about that?

Very. His heart might get a few palpitations when they kissed, his body definitely lusted after hers, his dreams were filled of images of Kristina, his hands always wanting to reach for her— but he would not get emotionally involved. He wasn't ready to stop roaming the world, saving injured people. He never would be as long as the nightmares about that night on the mountainside persisted.

Nick had never got to win gold at the skiing championships, hadn't fallen in love, or studied to become the architect he'd wanted to be, or had had children—all because his best friend hadn't been able to save him, try as hard as he did.

Sorry, Nick. So damned sorry.

Time to sign the contract that'd take him to another continent at the end of summer.

Chase dug his phone out and punched a number. 'Ethan, got a minute?'

'Sure. What's up?'

Not answering that. He shifted in his chair. 'Nothing. Just thought I'd give you a call.' No excuses needed this time. 'I could do with some sensible talk.'

'So Kristina's giving you grief. I like it.'

He should've left the phone in his pocket and sat on it. 'I don't.'

'We going to talk about this?'

Deep breath. 'I invited her to the farm. She turned me down.'

'Don't give up at the first knock, man. Be as stubborn about this as you are about work.'

'Like you?' Finally Chase began to relax. This was why he'd phoned his friend. 'I recall you opting to be there but not as a couple when Claire announced she was pregnant and keeping the baby whether you wanted it or not.'

'Watch and learn. If you want Kristina, go after her, be persistent until you win or lose.'

There was the million-dollar question. Did he want her? 'Yes.' The word sighed out of his throat. Yes.

CHAPTER SIX

'I'M GOING SHOPPING in Marseille tomorrow for my bridesmaid dress,' Kristina told Claire over the phone. 'I'll take photos if I find something special and email them to you for your approval.'

'Whatever you're happy with I'll like,' Claire replied. 'Have you docked already?'

'The city lights are getting closer by the minute.' She leaned on the rail in the space on deck and wished there was something more exciting to look forward to than buying a dress. Which was grossly unfair to her new friend. She dug deep for enthusiasm. 'Is sky blue still your colour of preference?'

'Unless you think you'll look hideous in it then yes. It's fashionable this season so it shouldn't be hard to find something.'

'If I don't have success here, I can try Nice or Genoa.'

'Remember to get something sexy, blow Chase's socks off. And his boxers.'

Kristina laughed hollowly. 'Yeah, right.' Her palm rubbed the scar line on her thigh.

'Kristina? Are you all right? Is something wrong?'

The concern in Claire's voice nearly undid her. 'I'm fine. Truly. With three days' leave about to start, why wouldn't I be?'

'Because you'll miss Chase.'

'Says who?'

'You weren't listening.' Claire paused. When Kristina neglected to fill in the silence, she continued, 'Still fancy him?'

'Yep.'

'The two of you need to get on with it, work whatever this is that you're denying out of your systems. Or make it something that's impossible to walk away from.'

This time Kristina was quick to speak, afraid of what else her friend might have an opinion on. 'Forget writing for an agony aunt column, you should try writing a romance. You've got the talent for making up stories.' Impossible to walk away from? She was already starting to think leaving Chase at the end of her twelve weeks was going to be hard.

This time Claire didn't laugh along with her. 'What's the problem? You're not sounding one hundred percent happy, so spill.'

Kristina glanced around, mindful Chase would

come out here once he'd finished his paperwork. She was alone. But then her extra-sensory perception had already told her that. Chase only had to step onto the deck and her body would thrum with excitement. 'He invited me to go home with him. it's his mother's birthday and there's a party planned.'

'That's wonderful. You'll have a great time. Don't you already know his sister and her family?'

'You weren't listening,' she remonstrated. 'I'm staying at the hotel MFA has booked in Marseille to go sightseeing and shopping.'

'Come on, Kristina. Take this opportunity to have some fun. As in real, let-your-hair down fun.' Her laughter was naughty and left nothing to Kristina's imagination about what that fun should be.

She wanted to agree, to accept Chase's invitation and enjoy herself without worrying about getting a job or finding the right dress for the wedding or whether she'd ever find a town to call home. But the consequences? Suddenly she said, 'I was hasty in turning him down.' Then hadn't known how to retract without showing Chase how her increasingly mixed emotions were screwing with her head.

'You're afraid of where it might lead, of being hurt. But you'll get nowhere if you don't take a chance. Look at me. I was afraid Ethan would walk away and now I'm planning a wedding and dealing with morning sickness every afternoon.'

'Whoa, slow down, will you? It's only a week-end with people I mostly don't know, not a love fest with a man who has me in the palm of his hand.' Scratch that last bit. He only had to look at her and she'd melt into a pool at his feet, into his arms, against that lean, muscular body.

'Stop holding back. Get out there and live a little.'

Could she do that without coming a cropper? She'd give up parts of herself for him, but not her need to be in control of her life. Going to Somerset with Chase would be like putting a match to petrol, and she'd grab it with both hands. It was the afterwards that frightened her. There were no guarantees. They might fall head over heels in love with each other and ride off into the sunset, or they could say that was good, thanks very much, and get on with the last three weeks on *SOS Poseidon*, but most likely she'd settle further into the depths of love beginning to spread through her head and her heart, and then she'd be lost. Unable to get back on track and finally make her life happen. 'It's not that simple, Claire.'

'Yes, it is. What have you got to lose that you haven't already?'

My heart. 'My sanity.'

'Sure you haven't already?' Claire asked in all seriousness. 'A little nudge in a different direction doesn't necessarily mean getting hurt, and it might find you something fabulous you've never expected.'

Kristina cut in. 'Don't you dare say look what happened to you two again.'

'I don't need to. You're already thinking about it. Now, a certain someone is indicating it's time to go for a stroll around the village before hitting the sack. Text me when you make up your mind about what you're doing.'

'I already told you.' But Kristina was talking to herself. The distinct sound of a phone being cut off was the only reply she got. *Thanks, friend.*

She stretched her legs one at a time, the left one protesting at the effort, then she stood with feet wide and bent over into the V pose of Downward Facing Dog. With her hands flat on the deck and her butt sticking up, she tried to clear her mind of everything but banishing the aches in her leg and back. She needed quiet space in her head to get back on track.

'I brought you tea.'

She whipped upright, wobbling on her feet as her head caught up with the sudden change from hanging down to being upright. Chase stood a metre away, holding two mugs, looking like he was caught in headlights. How long had he been there? Her cheeks burned. He should be in his office, not gaping at her rear end. 'I hoped you were giving this a miss tonight.'

He shook his head abruptly, and tea spilled onto the deck. His eyes were still too wide, and there was a distinct look of want turning them to forest green. 'I've finished the paperwork.' His voice had darkened. Sexy.

'Oh.' She hadn't got that message.

'That stretch helping?'

It had until he'd turned up. Though now she could forget the aches in her back and thigh because the tension in her stomach was taking over, sending pulses of heat to her core. She nodded, speech beyond her.

'Here.' He pressed a mug into her hand and turned to lean on the rail, his mug clasped in both hands as he stared across the narrowing gap between them and Marseille.

It was a miracle she didn't tip the tea all over the place. Her knuckles whitened and the mug steadied. Now what? Keep quiet and see what he said. That wasn't hard considering the block on her brain and the pounding in her chest.

'That's a beautiful sight.'

He was talking about the panorama before them, wasn't he? 'Cities look so exciting from a distance. All those lights have me guessing at what's going on in the streets.'

'Want to go see when we dock? We could have a drink in a wine bar or go to a jazz club.'

Definitely talking about the city. Not her butt. 'You're into jazz?'

'What's not to like about it?' He continued watching the approaching shoreline, like he didn't know where else to look.

'I wouldn't know.' Music wasn't her thing.

'Then it's time to find out.' He glanced at his watch. 'Meet me at the gangway in thirty.'

She hadn't seen that coming. 'You're on.' Just like that she had a date—with Chase Barrington. The only man she wanted to go out with. What to wear? Her pack hadn't come filled with dresses and fancy shoes, just T-shirts, shorts and sneakers. 'See you soon.'

She tore down the stairs. 'Jane,' she yelled as she shoved their cabin door wide. 'I need clothes to wear to a night club.'

'I've got a skirt that might fit you—don't dance too vigorously unless you want to show what you've got. Who are you going with?'

Kristina caught her breath and eyeballed her cabin mate, trying for stern. 'Chase.'

'Brilliant.' Jane held her hand up, palm out.

Caught up in the moment, Kristina raised her own hand, slapped Jane's in return. 'Let me see this skirt. And thanks. I'll have it back before you leave for your flight in the morning.'

'Don't worry. I can replace it in Monaco. It's not the prettiest skirt you'll have ever worn but it beats those denim shorts you're so fond of. Now, a top. We'll go and see Freja. She's got enough clothes to go round all the females on board.'

'Really? Why?'

Jane's laugh would've been heard all over the ship. 'She likes to be prepared. Why not when the men are falling all over her?' She knocked on a cabin door. 'Freja, you in there? We need help.'

Chase watched the vision coming towards him and felt the tension holding him stiff let go and a low whistle rush across his lips. 'You look stunning.'

Kristina grinned. 'Not a bad effort considering what was in my half of the shoebox-sized wardrobe.'

He held out his hand. 'Let's have some fun. I can't believe you haven't listened to jazz.' He couldn't believe they were going on a date.

Her fingers tightened around his. 'I'm open to new experiences.'

There was a plus. Though how many new ones they'd face tonight was anyone's guess. One step at a time. Chase blinked. How many steps did he plan on taking? He wasn't thinking only about tonight. But she'd already turned down his invitation for the weekend.

He waved down a taxi and helped Kristina inside, trying not to stare at her delightful derrière. But how could he not when it was right there; rounded, filling out the red skirt perfectly?

The jazz club was heaving when they arrived, standing room only and a queue for the bar. 'Welcome to downtown Marseille,' he said against her ear so he was heard. That he got a whiff of pine and roses was a bonus. 'What would you like to drink?'

'A mojito would be great.'

'Wait here, and I'll try to be quick.'

'I'm coming with you or we might never see each other again.' Her hand slid effortlessly back into his and she stayed close as they pushed through to the bar.

'There's a bar upstairs and one through that door,' the barman told Chase as he mixed Kristina's drink. 'Different bands at each and you might find some seating upstairs.'

'Merci,' Chase said. 'We'll take a look.'

The only available chairs were at a table with three other couples, who happily let them join the group. Chase settled Kristina before sitting beside her and propping his elbows on his knees, his chin in his hand. 'This is a jazz club.'

'No complaints so far.' She tossed him a saucy smile.

Was she flirting with him? Two could play

that game. 'I don't intend to give you anything to criticise,' he gave back, and felt strangely happy when she laughed.

'Sure of yourself, aren't you?'

'Oh, yeah.' What sort of man would admit to the butterflies that had come to life in the last minute? A woman didn't want an insecure guy trying to woo her. Wait, he was wooing her now? He sure was. Only for tonight. He'd see where they got to on mojitos and bourbon and loud music and hot moves on the dance floor. If they returned to the ship and separate cabins with the narrow uncomfortable bunks then that was how it would end. Standing, he held out a hand. 'Let's dance.'

'This could get tricky. These shoes aren't mine and they're a little tight.' But she was already heading for the dance floor, her hand pulling at his.

Chase couldn't take his eyes off her as she raised her arms and rolled with the music. She mightn't be familiar with jazz but her body certainly knew how to move. He felt clumsy beside her, his own movements heavy and awkward, and he'd thought he knew what he was doing on a dance floor. But it didn't matter. No one would be watching him, all eyes would be on his partner. But, boy, did she know how to swing those hips and push out her breasts and move her hands in time to the music that seemed to get louder and louder. He was lost. In her. In the picture before him. In the music that she was responding to as though she'd been dancing to jazz all her life.

When Kristina whirled around and wrapped her arms around his neck his hands found her slender waist and he leaned in to kiss her. Who needed bourbon when he had this woman in his grasp? She was an aphrodisiac in a tight skirt and low-cut top, balancing effortlessly on ladder-high heels. Chase tipped his head back and laughed. He had not been this happy in a long, long time.

Kristina heard that laugh, felt it all the way to her toes, and smiled around the bubble of excitement bouncing up her throat. This was Chase as she'd never seen him, letting go and relaxing, having fun, truly enjoying himself. With her. Right now life couldn't get any better. Right now was what it was about. Not yesterday. Not tomorrow. Tonight. Her hands gripped together at the back of his neck and she stretched up to kiss that teasing mouth, to put a stop to the rampant sensations his smile caused in her belly. Much more and they'd have to find a bed, fast.

As her mouth caressed Chase's, those sensations went into overdrive, spinning through her body, touching everywhere, bringing her alive beyond what she'd ever imagined. Yet her limbs still moved in time to the jazz filling the air.

Her feet hadn't stopped from the moment she'd walked onto the dance floor, while her eyes had been fixed on this sexy man holding her with those wicked hands, like he had no intention of letting her go. It felt like they were meant to be together, here, in this club, this city, on this night.

Then the lights flicked off then on again. A loud announcement broke through and brought her upright, still holding onto Chase, afraid to let him go in case that was the end of their time together.

'They're calling final drinks,' Chase interpreted. 'Let's get out of here and grab a taxi before the rush starts.'

She'd have hesitated, reluctant to go, but Chase took her hand in his and rubbed a thumb across the back, and her skin sat up to attention. 'All right.' Did he mean this wasn't the end of their night? 'We could walk. Our wharf's not too far away.'

'Are you sure your feet can stand it? Is your back playing up? You're walking a little lopsided.'

The concern in his voice touched her. She wasn't used to someone noticing and caring. Her back ached like mad and her thigh wasn't happy but she'd get over it. She was not spoiling a wonderful night by moaning about what couldn't be fixed. 'I don't want the night to end, that's all.'

'You're sure about that?' he asked.

'Absolutely.'

'I'm with you.' Chase pulled her up against him and kissed her forehead, then each cheek and finally, finally her mouth.

Oh, yes. She melted against him, kissed him back with all the passion pouring along her veins. So much for not getting involved. Right now there was nothing capable of stopping her. 'You're right. We need a taxi. Now,' she whispered from the side of her mouth, and went back to kissing him.

When she felt one arm lift from her shoulder she continued kissing him, pausing only to clamber into the cab and resume the instant Chase pulled her against him.

Then they were tipping out of the taxi at the security gate on the wharf. Kristina looked around. In the east the sky was beginning to lighten on the dark horizon. 'I can't remember the last time I was out all night.'

Chase placed an arm around her waist. 'I'd say you haven't been living, but it's the same for me. All work and no play makes for sad puppies.'

The guard waved them through. *'Bonsoir, Docteurs.'*

'Bonsoir, Louis.'

They reached the gangway. Chase murmured against her lips before his mouth covered hers, 'Come on. I can't wait any longer.'

'Chase, where the hell have you been?' a robust male voice interrupted them.

Chase ripped his mouth away from hers, though he kept his hands on her shoulders as she wobbled on those shoes, and asked the ship's captain, who was standing at the top of the gangway, 'What's the problem?'

'I've been phoning you for hours. Liam wants to talk to you urgently. He's in Manila and he isn't happy about something,' Josip told him.

The man was never happy about anything. Chase's hand automatically went to his pocket, pulled his phone free. 'Five missed calls.'

'You wouldn't hear it ringing inside the club. We couldn't hear ourselves think.' Not that she'd been doing much of that, unless it had involved the hot male body dancing before her. Hot and full of the promise of more heat. Kristina straightened, stepped back from those steadying hands, a sinking sensation going on in her stomach. Chase was back at work, whether he realised it or not, wanted to be or not. Being available twenty-four seven was what he did. Tonight had been uncharacteristic, not normal. She followed him up the gangway, trying not to drown in the disappointment flooding her.

He was telling Josip, 'I'm on leave. Have been since midnight.'

'Tell that to Liam. He's in a real mood, I'm warning you.'

Kristina reached the deck and stood watching Chase. The heat between them was gone, evaporated in a dose of reality. Though why should Chase let someone demand he phone them when he was on leave? But she already knew he would never walk away from his responsibilities. This was a timely reminder of how it would be if she took this any further. Her feet weren't yet back on the ground; she still wanted to follow through on their promises to go downstairs together. For her the night was not over. It might be out here where the sky was lightening to a grey shade of blue, but not within herself. No, her body was still afire with need. She laid a hand on his arm. 'Chase?'

Her heartbeat quickened as she watched the play of emotions on his face. Determination was winning. He was going to ignore Liam's calls and finish the night with her.

Then regret took over. 'Kristina, I'm sorry.'

'No, Chase. You don't have to be.' *You can come with me.* 'Phone Liam. I'll wait.'

He leaned in and kissed her. When he drew back his mouth lifted in a wry smile. 'I'll be as quick as I can. If I don't call back, Liam won't stop harassing Josip.'

Relief had her heartbeat slowly quietening. 'Remind Liam you have a life.'

'Unfortunately I don't really. Not outside MFA.' He leaned down to place the softest kiss ever on her lips. 'But for the first time I can remember, I want to. Thanks to you.'

'I'll be topside.' Could they make love in their space? Most personnel were long gone. No, most likely they'd head to Chase's cabin.

'See you shortly.'

She watched him stalk across to the stairway leading to his office, her hope of finishing the evening in his arms making love still there but cautious, uncertain. So much for having a great night out and then getting over him. All she wanted was more. 'Chase?'

He paused, turned back. 'Kristina?'

'Is your invitation to join you in Somerset still open?' Her heart stopped, her lungs waited.

Caution crept into his eyes. 'Yes, of course.'

Thump, thump. Breathe. 'Then I'll be at the gate at nine. What airline do I book a seat on?'

'Leave that to me. I'll do it while I'm talking to Liam.' The next thing she was being lifted up and swung around in a circle before being placed back on her feet and receiving another kiss, this time on the tip of her nose. 'Somerset, here we come.'

'Multi-tasking? But you're a man.'

'Glad you noticed.'

How couldn't she? 'I'll fix you up for the

flights.' They weren't in the sort of relationship where she'd accept him paying for her trip. Probably never would be. No reason not to have a load of fun over the weekend, though.

Up in 'their' space, Kristina toed off the shoes, which were killing her. It'd take more than one night to get used to glam footwear. Leaning on the railing, she soaked up the lights and tooting horns and shouts that was downtown Marseille at this hour, and let her excitement grow. How long would Chase be on the phone? Tempted to go down to his office and sit on his lap while he talked business, she wavered. That might be pushing the boundaries too far, too soon. One fantastic night would not change Chase into a relaxed, let's have fun with no consequences kind of guy. She hadn't changed that much either, and being tense and nervous would spoil the moment. She'd wait here, let the anticipation in her veins grow and keep her warm.

'Liam, what's so important you have to phone in the middle of the damned night?' Chase growled. The phone was on speaker to allow him to pace around the poky office, trying to pacify the tension in his body that was all about Kristina and her seductive body, and nothing to do with work.

'Interrupt something, did I?'

Damned right you did. The best thing that's happened in a long while. Like for ever.

Chase held back on shouting. Liam would wind him up relentlessly. When he didn't feel like killing the Swiss national, they were friends. 'I'm on leave and was out having a drink with friends.'

Make that a friend who's within minutes of being my lover.

'My apologies. I didn't think beyond needing to talk to you before you left for England.' Liam paused.

Chase didn't rush in to forgive him, just waited and paced.

'We've got a lot to do in the Philippines. The people here are in need of urgent medical help.'

Chase clicked onto the internet and the airline taking him home in a few hours. Might as well get Kristina's ticket sorted while listening to Liam's rant. Once he started there'd be no stopping him. Except this morning his call wasn't going to be a long diatribe. *He* had somewhere to go, a woman to be with, and frustration was making him edgy. He could feel Kristina under his hands, taste that sensational mouth on his lips, wanted, needed her body joined to his. 'Liam,' he snapped.

'I need you in two places at once. We're short of doctors. These people, Chase, they'd break your heart. Today I saw a three-year-old digging in the gutter for food. The boy needs urgent surgery for a displaced hip.'

The words came through the haze in Chase's head. There was a child who needed *him*. His skills. He pressed 'buy' on the flight details before him. 'You want me in Manila or Ghana next?' He'd be too late for the boy Liam was talking about. There were still weeks to go on the *Poseidon*, helping equally distressed people, but he'd go wherever he was most needed after that. It was why he was here, and would be there, or anywhere come tomorrow and all the days after.

Liam's sigh said it all. 'I guess Ghana. Who knows where you'll go after that? It's months away.'

'Whatever.' Chase saved Kristina's ticket, forwarded it to her phone. Kristina. She was waiting for him. Out in their space. 'I've got to go.' He wanted to make love with her. And then? Walk away? He stared at the screen where his copy of her ticket waited. There'd be no walking away for the next three days. And afterwards? After making love, and the party, and sharing his family, then what? Nothing would change. He still needed to save people.

Those demons still need to be placated, Nick. I can't stop moving from one crisis to the next. Can I?

Liam came through loud and clear. 'I don't like it when you go quiet. What's going on?'

'Sorry, doing two things at once.' It wasn't a lie, but it was the first time his mind was more focused on himself than on what Liam wanted. His gut churned with longing and the sense of missing out on something sensational. His trousers were uncomfortable, evidence of where his mind had been. Kristina.

'You need a break from all this? More than the three-day leave you've started?'

'Not at all.' But did he, though? The last nine weeks had knocked him around. First with Ethan landing in his life and insisting they sort out the past. That alone was enough to turn a man on his heel and have him running for the Sahara. Then along had come Kristina. Beautiful, mysterious, kind, fun and sexy. Don't forget the sexy. Like that was happening. She had his blood constantly running hot, and his ideas about his life sitting up and scratching at his head, as if to say, 'What am I doing? Do I want to spend the rest of my life going from one tragic place to another, to be always looking after those who can't look after themselves in faraway countries?'

Yeah, he did, because he had to.

'That's a relief.'

No pressure. He couldn't take any more. 'Talk

to you later.' Stabbing the 'off' button brought that conversation to an end. But no relief.

Tonight had started out as an evening of drinks and dancing and music, and had ended with kisses, and sex about to happen. Except they'd been interrupted. He should've ignored Josip and Liam. Then he wouldn't have been responsible for the disappointment that had filled Kristina's eyes and face and tugged at her shoulders when she'd realised he would put work before her. He'd said he'd join her on deck, but he'd also let her down. Hell, he'd let them both down.

Chase took the stairs two at a time. Kristina was waiting for him.

But she wasn't. The space was empty, only a hint of her scent to confirm she'd been here.

His heart plummeted. Did she believe he hadn't intended to join her? Why had she left? Looking around, he could see the outlines of bollards and chains. The sun was coming up. His watch showed it'd been nearly an hour since they'd parted at the top of the gangway. Really? Liam had talked for that long?

Kristina must have thought he wasn't coming to her.

He wanted to rail against her for not trusting him, but couldn't. He should've cut the conversation short and joined her, but he hadn't.

He couldn't let the night finish like this.

Couldn't. Sex was probably out, but an explanation—no, an apology was needed.

Kristina didn't answer his knock on her cabin door. The handle was locked.

Back in his office he texted her.

Liam took for ever.

No. He deleted the words, started again.

I am truly sorry. Can we try again? In Somerset? Airline tickets in your inbox.

Now he had a weekend to rectify things. If Kristina gave him a chance, which he so wanted. Of all the dumb things to have done, tonight's blunder had to be right up there. How close would he allow Kristina to get if she forgave him? Did they have a great time and walk away from each other come Sunday? Or did he give in to this crawling need coursing through his veins? For the first time in over a year he was going home, taking a woman with him who had his boxers in a twist and his heart holding its breath.

For the first time ever he was beginning to feel there was more to life than sick people in need of him. And it was scary.

CHAPTER SEVEN

'I'VE PREPARED YOU the bedroom next to Chase's,' Verity Barrington told Kristina much later. 'I wasn't sure if you two were friends or something more, so I've covered the bases.'

Kristina squirmed under the older woman's scrutiny. Was a man's mother supposed to say things like that?

There was a twinkle in Verity's eye that did nothing to quieten the hope knocking softly in Kristina's heart. It had started when Chase had apologised deeply as they'd waited for the taxi to take them to Marseille Province airport and it became real when his father, Alec, pulled up in front of the large double-storeyed farmhouse in Somerset and she'd climbed out of the four-wheel drive to stare around, with Chase standing beside her. The green fields where sheep grazed and the large implement sheds where tractors and machinery were stored made her feel she'd done the right thing in coming here. She was spending a weekend in Chase's territory.

'Watch out,' Chase had warned when German shepherds had charged out to greet first him and then her, making her welcome. His parents had accepted her without a barrage of questions, even hugged her on introduction. But that hope lurking in Verity's eyes when she'd mentioned the sleeping arrangements had Kristina questioning if she'd done the right thing in coming here.

'Thank you so much. I really appreciate you having me to stay.' She wasn't saying a word about bedrooms. For one, she didn't know the answer herself, and, secondly, Chase would put her on the next flight out if she talked about him to his mother.

'This couldn't get further from my cabin. It's enormous and I'm not sharing with Jane, who snores like a hungry pig. Nor are there people all over the place needing attention and fearful of asking for it.'

'It must get quite intense, dealing with those poor people.' Verity's eyes turned in the direction of her son, who was sitting in the conservatory with his father now that dinner was over. 'I know it takes a toll on Chase. Not that he's ever admitted it, but we see it in his demeanour. He's always tired, and doesn't laugh as much as he once did.'

'He takes his work very seriously.'

'Too seriously. While I'm not saying it's wrong, it breaks my heart that he doesn't lighten up a little. It's as though he doesn't want to enjoy life to its fullest.'

Kristina knew exactly where she was coming from. However, it wasn't her place to get involved in a deep and meaningful discussion about Chase. 'It's hard to put aside the things we see on a daily basis, which is why we have these breaks. They're essential to coping.'

'How long have you been on board the *Poseidon*?'

'I've done nine weeks, with three to go before I return to England and find a permanent job.'

'I wish Chase would do something similar.'

How long had it been since this woman had talked about her son to someone other than family? Why choose her? Hadn't she got the message that there wasn't a relationship going on, even if they were spending the weekend together? 'I'm sure he knows what he's doing,' she said softly, trying not to sound critical. The last thing she wanted was for Verity to turn her back on her. She liked the woman, and not just because she was Chase's mother. She was a charming, warm soul who adored her family and made strangers feel comfortable.

'I'll make a pot of tea. Would you like a cup?' Disappointment clouded the older woman's face.

Regret at having cut Verity off, but having had to before the conversation got out of hand, Kristina smiled. 'I'd love one. Shall I ask the men if they want one?'

'Alec will, but I don't know about Chase.' It was obvious she didn't know a lot of things about her son any more.

So he'd cut himself off from his family in order to stay true to his goal of saving people. Didn't he understand he could do that by living and working full time in Somerset? In the same country even? Saving people didn't mean only those who were in jeopardy of their lives because of politics. Helping a young girl overcome pain from a broken leg was as rewarding as removing a melanoma from a man's back before it metastasised.

'Where have you gone?' Chase stood in front of her.

She shook her head. 'I was coming to ask if you wanted a cup of tea.' Then, before he could ask more and she'd have to lie, she added, 'I'm looking forward to seeing more of the farm.'

'You ever been on one?'

'A couple of times when I was at boarding school I went home for long weekends with a girl who's a distant cousin. I didn't like the horses, too big and scary. But the cows and farm dogs were all right. More importantly, I loved the wide open spaces and how I could yell and laugh and no one heard me.'

'I'll take you to the farthest field tomorrow.'

'Or you could wait until the grandkids get here and they can compete with Kristina.' Alec laughed. 'Those kids don't know the meaning of quiet.'

'I can't wait to see them again.' She meant it. It would be interesting to watch Chase interacting with them, too. Aloof, or down on his knees, hugging and playing, like he did on the ship? Could he remain uninvolved with them? Or would they knock his memories and fears aside for a short while? 'I met the boys at the medical centre. They certainly know how to create havoc.'

'Sounds like my nephews.' Chase grinned.

Suddenly Kristina's body slumped with exhaustion and it was hard to concentrate. A lack of sleep and being on edge about coming here was taking its toll. Now she'd relaxed everything was catching up. 'I know it's early but I think I'll go to bed, if no one minds.'

'Of course not. Take your tea with you,' Verity said. 'Make yourself at home and don't hesitate to use anything you want.' It was what any good hostess would say but it came with a huge dollop of kindness.

Kristina's eyes watered, and it took strength not to throw her arms around the woman. But she didn't. It might make her seem needy. Which she probably was. Why hadn't her mother been half as loving? Or her father? They did love her. They just had never shown it in the way she needed. It had been there in the trust funds and the expensive education her father had paid for, and the holidays to the luxury apartments her mother lived in with her latest billionaire. They didn't understand she'd have swapped it all for hugs and being cuddled when the cat died and having them watch when she acted in the school play. 'Goodnight, everyone.'

She scarpered to her room before emotion got the better of her, making her act like a blithering idiot. Coming here was beginning to look like a mistake.

'Kristina, wait,' Chase called as she began to close the bedroom door. 'Are you all right?' He leaned an arm against the doorframe, studying her closely.

'Why wouldn't I be? Your parents are lovely.'

'So it's not their fault you're about to burst into tears?' His smile was gentle and undid the final cord holding in her emotion.

'No way,' she managed as those now familiar arms closed around her and drew her against the broad chest she'd touched last night. Why did she have to get so emotional? 'They're so open and friendly. It's not what I expected since they don't know me.'

'They're always like that, especially Mum. So, now what? Do I walk to my room and forget you're upset? Or shall I stay here and kiss you better?'

Kristina stepped backwards, her arms now firmly holding Chase, not wanting to let him go anywhere but up against her in her room. 'Option two.' She was only referring to a kiss, wasn't she? Yes, she had to be. For the sake of her head and heart. Not that she'd given those a thought last night when they'd been speeding back to the ship.

Bending towards her, Chase brushed his lips across hers and drew back a little. 'What made you sad?'

'Don't talk. Please,' she added, breathless around the electricity zipping throughout her body. Placing her mouth on his to shut him up and abate that current now debilitating her, she closed her eyes and went with the kiss. Went with being lost in Chase's arms, letting go of everything else, aware only of them.

A groan erupted between them, and opening her eyes she saw the happiness on Chase's face, in his eyes, and was happy to have given him that…and because his hands were circling her waist and his broad chest pressing against her breasts and awakening her further.

Kristina ripped her mouth away from his and stared at him. Making love was moments away— if she gave in to what she was feeling. It would be as easy as taking two steps and sinking onto the bed. She wanted it, needed Chase naked against her, pushing into her, taking her to great heights. And yet… 'Can we talk? I mean, I don't think I'm ready.'

His thumb rubbed across her lips. 'Damn.' He smiled. 'But it's okay. I think I understand.'

'I don't,' Kristina admitted, reluctant to remove her hands from him, wanting his strength and warmth. She backed away. 'I'm sorry.'

There was confusion and something she couldn't identify in his gaze. His voice was rough when he replied, 'Don't be. You're being honest, as you always are.'

If she was honest she'd admit to being afraid of where this could lead, scared of having her heart broken, of being left alone again. Better not to have loved than to love and lose him. Yet all she wanted was to fall onto the bed with Chase in her arms and forget the nagging memories from the past, to believe in a future filled with hope. She'd had time to think about this on the flight. She looked at him long and hard. If only she had the guts to follow through on the longing filling her from head to toe. If only. Early that morning nothing would've stopped her. What a difference a day could make. 'Goodnight, Chase,' she whispered.

'See you in the morning.' But he didn't move,

remained standing there, watching her, a question in his eyes.

'What?' she asked finally.

He shook his head. 'It doesn't matter.'

The door clicked shut behind him and she was left feeling that she'd missed something big. 'I'm sorry,' she whispered.

She'd been looking out for herself. Sinking onto the bed, she hugged herself tight. And cursed silently. The more she came to know Chase the more she believed he was right for her—if he wasn't so determined to be alone. Not that Verity had intended to but she'd reminded Kristina of the reasons she shouldn't fall in love with him. If it wasn't already too late. Double whammy, that. If this emotion that kept flooring her, stalling her was love, she'd found it with the wrong man. It had sneaked up and snared her when she wasn't looking.

Crawling into bed, she tugged the covers up to her chin and concentrated on forgetting Chase and his potent kisses, tried to think about the email she'd received from Jarrod that morning, asking if she'd drop into the medical centre tomorrow and catch up with everyone. There was something he wanted to discuss with her. Could there be a position going in Merrywood? A permanent one? If there was, how did she feel about it? Ha, that was one thing she did know the answer to.

It was exactly what she wanted, would be the perfect opportunity to get on with her life. She knew the staff, liked the locals, and could buy a cottage to suit her needs. She'd live alone. She'd meet people, and maybe a man would come along she would fall in love with.

Chase.

No, not Chase. She should never have come here. Now she had something else to put behind her.

Could be that she was getting ahead of herself. Jarrod might only want to catch up and offer her more locum work. And these feelings for Chase might be a figment of her overactive imagination.

Chase got up with the sun to take the dogs for a walk along the lane leading around the copse behind the house. So much for catching up on sleep. Impossible when Kristina reigned supreme in his head.

They'd come close to falling into bed together. So close he could still taste it on his tongue, feel it in his veins. But she'd backed off. That had nearly crushed him. He'd wanted her very badly, and he'd have sworn she felt the same. If not for Liam's phone calls the night before, they would've made love in his cabin. He'd have touched her everywhere, tasted her skin, felt her need, and held her to him as he pressed into her. He'd have known her intimately.

But he hadn't, though he wanted to more than ever. But he'd never force her to do something she wasn't one hundred certain about. Kristina had to come to him willingly. And had to want to make love as much as he wanted her. That was the scary thing. Because he did want Kristina, all of her, so damn much it hurt. He longed for the lovemaking, the laughter, the sadness, the history—and then a future.

'A future?' he roared at the blue sky looking down on him.

The dogs leapt, stared at him, their legs tense and shaking.

'Sorry, boys, but you don't know what it's like to be so damned afraid of grasping the chance at a future that might be on offer.' If only he could find the guts to front up to Kristina and lay these mixed-up feelings before her.

What do you reckon, Nick? Am I being stupid to think there might be a future with Kristina?

His head moved rapidly from side to side. It couldn't happen. That'd be a disaster. The desire crawling through his veins would become love, and he couldn't honour that in the way Kristina deserved. She needed a man at her side all the time, not when it pleased him to come home.

She was not interested in travelling to different countries to put her medical skills to good use and he could not imagine himself staying in one place for ever. See? They were poles apart in their needs, and those poles could not be moved closer. He knew this in his bones. Nick was in the way.

The cool morning air made Chase shiver. Or could it be the sense of loss washing over him? Strange, when what he might be losing he hadn't actually gained in the first place. Deep conversations and off-the-scale kisses, a night on the town in a jazz club—that did not add up to a full-on relationship where both of them gave everything of themselves. Kristina had demons, too, but she was trying to work through them, unlike him.

Chase picked up his speed. He'd prepare breakfast, save his mum time when she already had plenty to do for the party.

'Woof, woof.' The dogs began trotting faster.

'Smell a rabbit, do you?' He turned and the air stuck in his throat.

Kristina stood in the ankle-high grass, hands clasped at breast height as she swung left and right from the waist, that stunning light hair, free for once and swishing back and forth across her back.

His mouth dried. 'OMG…' What little air was in his lungs hissed over his lips. Parts of his anatomy went rock hard. He couldn't move but he had to or she'd see him staring and think he was perving. He was. Couldn't help himself. 'Kristina,' he gasped. When she didn't acknowledge him he tried to swallow. It was impossible when his mouth was like a desert. Putting one leg in front of the other, he closed the gap, tried again. 'Morning, Kristina.'

Her eyes flew open and her arms fell to her sides. 'No wonder I couldn't rouse you. You were already out here.'

'You're up early.'

'Old habits. I never sleep late.'

Not lack of sleep because of thinking about how they could've spent the night together? Her eyes were puffy and dull. He sighed. They weren't doing each other any favours. 'Neither do I. I'm heading back to do something about breakfast.'

'Verity's got it in hand. She said it would be ready in forty-five minutes and not to be late. I thought I'd limber up with a few yoga exercises before taking a short walk.'

'Want company?' He held his breath.

'I'd love it.'

Chase breathed again. 'We'll head to the top of the copse, then follow the track that comes out behind the farmhouse.'

'This place is wonderful. You were lucky to grow up here.'

'I know.' He tried not to stare at her butt filling those tight denim shorts as she strolled along, but his eyes had a mind of their own—until he tripped over a sod of grass-covered soil and nearly fell flat on his face. What had they been talking about? Oh, yeah. 'As kids Libby and I used to raise any calves rejected by their mothers for one reason or another. We had to do all the work and when they were sold at market we received half the money. The rest went to Dad to cover costs, though he was soft and didn't hit us with a large share of the expenses.'

'He was teaching you that nothing comes to you without working for it. I like that. My parents, especially Mum, thought the more they gave me the more I'd love them and not argue about who to stay with during the school holidays.' Kristina stopped to look around. 'Luxuriant green for miles and miles.'

Following the direction of Kristina's gaze, he admitted, 'I don't always see it like that. It's a big part of me, and still I don't get lost in being here.'

Drawing her eyes away from the view, she started walking again. 'You obviously weren't meant to be a farmer. Did that bother your father?'

'Dad's never been anything but encouraging in what ever I chose to do. This farm hasn't been in the family for generations like some around here.

It was Dad's dream, and he went after it with everything he had. Then let his children follow their own dreams. I think he's hoping one of Libby's boys might be interested, but they're a few years off making those kinds of decisions.'

'The freedom of it all.' The wistful note in Kristina's voice caught at him.

'What did your parents want from you?' She can't have let them down by becoming a GP.

'Nothing I was prepared to give my soul for.' She strode out, leaving him behind.

Chase lengthened his steps and caught up. 'I hope you like a full English breakfast, because Mum's not going to let you away with anything less.' He wasn't going to follow up on that terse comment. There'd been pain in every word, pain she wasn't ready to share. Hopefully one day she'd find it in her to tell him. If he was still in the same country as her. Which wasn't going to happen so he wouldn't be hearing about her parents and how they'd raised her.

'My mother thinks marrying a millionaire is the only way to go.' Her laugh was tight. 'Lying by a pool for a couple of days a year is fine, doing it year round isn't my idea of fun.'

'I can't see you filling in time for the sake of it.' Surprised she'd given him a snippet, he waited to see if there was more.

'Dad wanted me to work with him, his company's specialty being hedge funds.'

Chase chuckled. 'Sitting in a high-rise, glass-encased office making millions online to please wealthy men who own fancy yachts isn't you either.'

'Dad isn't any good at knowing what makes me tick.' Again sadness tainted her voice.

And made him want to cheer her up. 'Do you want a lift into Merrywood this morning? I hear Jarrod wants to catch up with you. We could have lunch at the pub afterwards.' He was getting the hang of this dating caper.

Her mouth curved upward. 'Family, eh? Knows everything about everyone?' Then she blanched. 'I didn't mean I was part of your family.'

'Relax, Kristina,' he said, hating the worry clouding her eyes, wanting to see any other emotion there, even anger, toward him. 'No one's expecting more of you than to enjoy the time we're here and to join in all the fun.'

She suddenly grinned, a bright light in the cloud that had fallen over her. 'I'd like a ride into town, and especially lunch with you.'

With you. Two simple words and his chest was filling with pride and excitement. 'You'll be doing me a favour. Mum has a list a mile-long of groceries, meat, flowers and a million other things that need to be picked up.'

Her knuckles rapped his upper arm lightly. 'My shout at the pub.'

'It's a deal.' His blood warmed, his heart squeezed. Was this a second date with Kristina? So what if it was? He'd promised to have a good time, and not think about the future. 'We'll leave straight after breakfast.'

'I need to hit the shops. I haven't got anything to wear to the party.'

'Now she tells me,' he groaned. 'Is this going to take all day? Or are you a speed shopper?' Then it struck him as odd that she had no clothes for anything other than work. 'You must own more clothes than the shorts and shirts you carry in that backpack.'

'There's a wardrobeful at my father's Manchester apartment where I have a bedroom I use about once a year. Mostly it's for storing my gear. Another reason for finding a town to settle in, a home to live in. I'll be able to buy furniture I like, clothes I'll wear more than once before putting them in storage, collect recipe books and serving dishes.' She gathered a breath. 'Cooking isn't my strong point, mainly because I've never done any. Put that on my sheet of things to do—when I start one—take lessons on how to make duck *à l'orange* or tortellini in smoked mussel sauce.'

'You don't want to start with porridge or

ginger-nut biscuits?' His mother had insisted he learn to make basic meals because cooking was her passion. Kristina obviously hadn't been given the chance. Because there'd been servants? Or no one could be bothered or patient enough to take the time to walk her through a recipe?

'Why start at the bottom?' She grinned in that way of hers that hit him in the gut and rattled his bones.

'Fair enough.' He opened the gate before them and breathed her in as she went through, her arm brushing his. 'Follow this path and we'll be through the trees and at the back door in minutes. Hopefully we haven't kept the bacon waiting.' What would that hair feel like on his skin?

Kristina felt a nudge in her belly as her arm brushed Chase's. Her feet tangled and she stumbled. Why hadn't she made love with him last night? She'd spent every hour until the sun rose regretting her decision.

'Careful.' Chase's hands caught and steadied her. His thumbs drew leisurely circles against her skin. His mouth was close, so close.

She had to kiss him, to feel his heat. 'Chase,' she whispered against his stubble-covered chin before her lips touched his. 'Chase.'

'Hell, Kristina, I've been wanting to do this since I saw you in the field.'

Her mouth peeled away far enough for her to reply, 'Good,' before she returned to kissing, this time trailing a line from the corner of his mouth to his chin and down his neck to the edge of his shirt. She yanked the shirt up and continued the kisses over his chest, down to his stomach where her tongue circled his belly button. They should've done this last night, she thought. Well, she wouldn't be stopping for anything this time.

'Those shorts should be banned. They cradle your butt like my hands need to. They outline your slim legs to the point that if I don't touch them, I'm going to die.'

'Help yourself,' she murmured against his stomach, while her hand sought the button holding his shorts closed and preventing access to the hard rod of need she had to touch, to wrap her hand around.

Chase groaned against her as she worked the button free.

Then his hands were on her pants, trying to push them down. 'Here.' She shoved his hand aside and tore the zip open, before returning to Chase's throbbing reaction to her. Reaching inside, her hands found him and slipped slowly down the satin skin stretched tight. She gasped at the wonder of his hardness, the heat, the throbbing need for her.

He dropped to his knees, his mouth finding

her. Kristina gripped his shoulders, her head tipping back as Chase licked and nipped first one thigh and then the other. As his mouth reached the puddle of desire making her shake, her fingers grabbed his head, clung to him as he touched her, a lick, then another, and another, and she melted and tightened and let go all at once as hot, hungry need rocked her.

Chase rose before her, and gently laid her in the thick grass. His eyes were dark and intense, his erection throbbing when she enclosed it in her hands. She had to have him inside her. 'Now,' she cried.

Chase held himself above her. Winding her legs around him, she drew him down until his tip touched her. When she gasped he pushed, slowly, firmly, inside. Withdrew, pushed in. Her arms, wrapped around his shoulders, convulsed in time with her need exploding around him. Chase pushed hard, shuddering as he came.

Slowly her heartbeat returned to normal. Tipping her head back, she drew a long, unsteady breath. 'Wow.'

'Yeah, wow.' Chase rolled onto his back, sprawling her across him.

She clung to him, absorbing his heat. 'Guess we're officially late for breakfast now.'

'I don't think Mum will be too worried. She doesn't start cooking eggs until everyone's seated at the table. But we'd better get a wiggle on or there'll be a load of unwanted questions to deal with. If the dogs haven't already told them what's going on.'

Kristina laughed as she scrambled to her feet. 'What dogs?'

'Exactly.' Chase took her hands in his. 'What happened to "I don't think I'm ready"?'

'I spent the night regretting it.'

His smile devoured her. 'I nearly knocked on your door at three this morning.'

'It took till three?'

'Nah. I was playing hard to get, but it back-fired.'

Winding her arm around his waist, she smiled for the short distance to the house, and then in her room where she quickly tidied up, and through-out breakfast, subtly ignoring Verity's amused glances coming their way. She was not sorry she'd made love with Chase. No, all she wanted was to do it again. Unfortunately the day ahead was about preparing for a party and catching up with everyone at the medical centre. Not that that was a bad way to spend a day, it was just that now she knew there was an even better one.

CHAPTER EIGHT

'KRISTINA, YOU'RE HERE.' The medical centre's receptionist flew around the counter and engulfed her in an enormous hug.

Kristina's heart melted at the welcome. She felt like crying. 'Hey, Wendy, good to see you.'

'You're in time for morning tea. Libby sent blueberry muffins in with Jarrod.'

More tears threatened. Kristina straightened her back and dropped her hands to her sides. 'I am being spoilt.'

'Watch out, they want something from you,' Chase teased. 'Believe me, I know how this lot operate.'

'Dr Kristina, hello. Do you want to see my baby? She weighed in at four kilos and hasn't stopped gaining weight since.' A young woman held up a baby dressed in pink and held her out. 'We called her Lily.'

'Sherry, it's lovely to see you both.' Kristina took the soft bundle in her arms. 'Hello, little one. Aren't you the cutest thing? Look at all those blonde curls.' In the weeks Kristina had worked there she'd seen Sherry regularly.

'Lily came in a real hurry and I didn't make it to hospital.' Sherry was smiling, her eyes full of love as she gazed at her daughter.

Kristina's stomach turned to goo. *I want that.* Handing Lily back, she managed, 'I'm so glad to see you both. I really am.' There was a sense of completing a circle, something that didn't usually happen for a locum.

'Me, too,' Sherry acknowledged. 'You were so kind to me when I panicked and cried for hours about my swollen ankles.'

'It was only minutes and every pregnant woman is allowed those moments.'

'Hello, Kristina. It's great to see you. Libby'll be along shortly. She's bursting to catch up on everything you've done since leaving here.'

Kristina turned to find herself slap bang in the middle of another hug, this time from Jarrod. When she was released she asked, 'Is she at the market?'

Jarrod nodded. 'Otherwise she'd be on to the list I presume is burning a hole in Chase's pocket. Come through to the tearoom where everyone's waiting.'

'But it's Saturday.' Merrywood Medical Centre had obviously been rostered to cover weekend emergencies for the area, but that didn't explain all the staff.

'They weren't letting you get away without seeing them.'

'Oh.'

Chase was biting on a smile. 'I prefer chocolate muffins so I'll leave you to it. Mum's list will take some effort to get through.'

'I said I'd help with it.' Kristina didn't want to let him down.

'I'm not tramping around behind you while you trawl the dress shops. Pick you up here at twelve-thirty, okay? We'll have lunch, then I'll put you to good use working on what's left of the list.'

'Sounds good.' Hopefully there'd be an outfit for the party in the first shop she went into. If there was spare time, she'd look for a sky-blue, full-length dress as well.

'Thanks for coming in when I know it's bedlam at the farm.' Jarrod led the way into the tearoom, where two nurses hugged her.

Were the hugs adding up this morning, or what? 'Verity's got everything under control, no sign of panic. How's everything here? I've missed this place.'

'Give this lot five minutes and then we'll go through to my office. Thankfully it's not too busy for a Saturday morning so we'll have some time to ourselves.'

Interesting. A fizz of excitement tickled her, and made the next five minutes the longest she could remember even when feeling so welcome.

'Bring your coffee.' Jarrod was on his feet and heading out the door.

As Kristina took a seat in his office the mug shook in her hand. Tension tightened her stomach. Was she about to get the offer of a lifetime or be sorely disappointed?

'Hey, there you are,' Libby bounded into the room and banged the door shut behind her before embracing Kristina. 'I'm glad you came with Chase for the weekend. It's great to see you again.'

This was getting out of hand. Kristina hugged her back fervently. 'Me, too. I thought you were selling cheese this morning.'

'I have been, but a friend's taken over. Jarrod wants me here while he talks to you. Probably thinks I can twist your arm for him.'

She straightened her back. This meeting was serious, then. *Please, be what I'm hoping for.* She waited, her breath stalled in her throat.

'I'll cut straight to the point. Campbell's leaving us, heading to New York where his wife's got a power job at some financial conglomerate.'

Kristina relaxed a notch. 'No surprise there. She's supposedly a whiz at that stuff. But can Campbell practise in the States?'

'He'll have to sit some papers, but he's decided

to be a stay-at-home dad until the kids have settled into their new way of life, which will be very different from little old Merrywood.' Jarrod steepled his fingers. 'So, are you still looking for a permanent position as a GP? Because there's one going here and we'd like you to join us. Everyone would. You were so popular with the staff and patients during your two months, and I'm tired of patients asking when you're coming back.'

Lay on the feel-good stuff, why don't you? A smile split her face. 'I do want to work in a medical centre where I get to know patients for more than one visit.' Come on, say what you really think. 'Okay, truly? Merrywood feels right for me, and I would like to move here.'

Jarrod was watching her closely. 'Campbell intends to hold onto his partnership for now, in case things don't work out in New York. But even if he returns, this position is permanent. Our patient numbers are high, and could grow more if we opened the books again.'

'I don't need a partnership.' Maybe later on when she was settled in her own home with those dogs she'd begun thinking about. What about Chase? He was the snag in this otherwise perfect solution to her needs.

'Say yes, Kristina,' Libby said.

'So you're interested in working with us? Permanently?' Jarrod asked, before dangling a carrot in front of her. 'Campbell has suggested that whoever takes his place here might be interested in renting their home.'

That would take the pressure off finding her own place, give her time to look around and decide where best to put down roots. Kristina stared at her entwined fingers, looking for the answer to the main question, because now the offer had come, there were other things to consider.

These people were Chase's family. Libby and Jarrod lived nearby, his parents a few kilometres down the road. He'd come home for visits, even if only occasionally, and she'd have to deal with seeing him, unless she took annual leave whenever he appeared. Despite the high she was on from that morning's lovemaking, come the end of her time with MFA their fling would finish. And it was definitely a fling. Chase was not ready for anything else.

Lifting her head, she looked at Libby, then Jarrod. 'Thank you so much for this opportunity. It's exactly what I want.' Deep breath. 'But there are things I need to consider. Can I have a few days before I give you my answer?'

Jarrod nodded. 'I didn't expect anything less. Just know that you're wanted around here by everyone, and that we'll all do whatever we can to help you settle in.'

'You're off to a head start, knowing my family,' Libby pointed out.

The snag in this whole deal. 'True, but I also have a need to see myself sorted, to find my feet. This would be a permanent move, and I want to get it right.'

'No problem.' Jarrod glanced at his computer and stood up. 'Sorry to rush you but I've a patient waiting.' He handed her an envelope. 'We haven't talked hours or salary, but it's all in there. Any questions or uncertainties, give me a call, or talk to me over the weekend.'

'I will.' She stood, surprised to find her legs a little shaky. Was this what finally finding what she wanted in life felt like? But it wasn't everything she hoped for. Until Chase, falling in love, possibly having a family, had been a distant dream to be followed when all else was in place and going well. Now she couldn't imagine life without Chase and yet that was exactly how it would be.

Libby slipped an arm through hers. 'Come and have another coffee, then we'll go to my favourite clothing shop because I hear you need an outfit.'

Two friends now? Special women she could talk to about anything. Except she couldn't with Libby because she had a brother who'd made love with her only hours ago, who no doubt would again before the weekend was up, and who, in the

end, would walk away from her. No, she wouldn't
be talking with Libby about what mattered. Unfortunately. But they could have fun shopping.

Sunday dawned wet and misty, and Kristina
couldn't have cared less. Chase had taken her to
his bed after the party had wound down and she
was still there. He had one leg thrown over hers
like he never wanted her to leave. That was an
illusion, like the one that said summer was only
about sun and warm temperatures.

'What are you looking so happy about?' Chase
nuzzled against her neck.

'That was some party.' She grinned.

'The Barringtons are famous for putting on a
good bash.' He was watching her now.

'I'll 'fess up. The after-party bash was even
better.' Leaning over, she kissed his chin, felt the
rough texture of beard growth.

'Glad you mentioned it. My ego was getting a
little worried.'

'I'm glad I came. To the party,' she added as
a grin began widening his beautiful mouth. 'It's
been quite a weekend so far.'

'A great party, amazing sex, and then there's
Jarrod's offer. What more could a woman want?'

'There is that.' The air dribbled out of her
lungs, taking some of her happiness with it. To
accept the job was the right thing to do. Yet she

still hoped for something more with Chase. And if that wasn't possible then living in this district might encroach on his hopes for the future. Not that she could say why, but she did think that if she moved here he might stop visiting entirely and she wouldn't be responsible for that.

'Hey, if you don't want it, say so. You're not obligated to Jarrod.' Chase sat up and tucked an arm over her shoulders, drawing her close.

Why couldn't he see what they had? This easy rapport, a simple gesture of holding her, a kiss on his chin as they woke to a new day. 'We'd better get up. Your mother will need all hands on cleaning-up duties.' Kristina swung her legs out of the bed.

Chase took his time removing his arm from around her. 'You're avoiding my question. Haven't we moved past that?' He shook his head. 'Spill. What's bothering you?'

This so wasn't the time. But when would it be? Twisting to face him, she placed a hand on his arm, felt his strength and warmth. 'The job is perfect, the location is ideal, the future looks good.'

'But?'

No. She couldn't say she was falling for him. He'd shut down completely, and she wanted what was left of their time together. Today at least. Call her selfish, but this sense of belonging had never come along before. Why not make the most of what little time she had left? *Am I being greedy?* Yep.

'I get a little scared when I think about how lucky I am to have this opportunity. It's what I've been looking for and I'm scared it'll be snatched away. Part of me thinks if I don't say yes to Jarrod yet, the bubble won't burst too soon.' Now he'd think she was mad, but she always told him the truth—about most things. Those she didn't she avoided.

Chase's arms wrapped around her and drew her close. His lips caressed her brow, then trailed down to her mouth where he kissed her softly. 'Believe in yourself, Kristina. If this is what you want then grab it with both hands and never let go. You're strong because of what you've faced in the past. Draw on that strength. Keep on smiling and winning people over because that's also helped get you to where you can make a decision about your future.'

Tears streamed down her face. See? No wonder she loved him. Yes, full-blown love. That falling for him thing had arrived at its destination. She loved Chase Barrington. So tell him. Always truthful, remember? Avoidance, remember? She didn't need him saying, 'Thank you very much but nothing's going to change'. Her pride had taken enough knocks over the years to know

when to look out for herself. Now was one of
those times.

'Thank you.' She sniffed. 'I needed that.' If
only she could give the same back. But they
weren't talking about him and his plans after
the *Poseidon*. Hopefully she'd get an opportunity over the next three weeks to do something
about that. Who knew? She might even find the
courage to tell him how she felt about him.

'Any time.' He grinned. 'Now, go shower.
There's a party to clear up.'

Chase watched Kristina head out of his bedroom,
his heart heavy despite that grin he'd given her.
Go, Jarrod, for offering her the position at the
medical centre. It was exactly what she wanted,
and needed. She'd be mad not to accept. So why
the hesitation? He didn't believe her explanation.
Or rather he did, but it was only half the reason.
What was the other half? He'd wanted to push
for an answer but was wary of spoiling the wonderful time they were having together.

They'd be flying back to Marseille in the afternoon. No wonder he felt dispirited. He wasn't
ready to go back to work, and that was such a
rarity. He put his hand on his brow. Temperature
normal. He and Kristina had hit it off so well the
idea of giving it up so soon rankled. Hell, he'd
come to enjoy her in his space, not only on the

ship but also here amongst his family. She was special. Could they have a relationship after all? One that went beyond this weekend, further than the next three weeks on board the ship, out into the real future?

Chase leapt out of bed and snatched up his shirt. Pulling it over his head, he grabbed his shorts and jerked them up his legs. Time to give his mum a hand downstairs. He'd shower after all the hard work of packing up chairs and tables and taking down the marquee was done.

'Where do you want me to start, Mum?' Chase sauntered into the kitchen minutes later, a tight smile fixed in place.

'With eating breakfast,' he was told. 'Then you can do a rain dance in reverse, get the sun to beat away those pesky clouds and dry everything out.'

'Sure thing.' He hugged the woman who'd been there for him all his life, had never backed away when he'd lost his mind over Nick's death, who still believed in him no matter what he did and how often he hurt her. His throat started closing as he said, 'Happy birthday, Mum. You're the best mother a guy could have.'

She blinked, patted his face and said, 'I'm the only one you've got, that's why.' Then she smiled that special mum smile that always hit him hard, especially since the tragedy that had changed his life for ever. 'You're my best son, too.'

'I'm the only one,' he croaked the expected reply, and pulled her into another hug.

'Come on, you two. Haven't got all day to be mucking about, real birthday or not.' His dad strolled into the kitchen and dropped onto his usual chair, pulled the pan of bacon towards him and began dishing some onto a plate.

Chase sank onto a chair and tugged the dish out of his father's hand. 'You reckon?' Then the air crackled around his ears, the skin on his forearms tightened.

Kristina had arrived. 'That smells so good, Verity.'

'Help yourself, and don't be mean about it. You're going to be so busy you'll need all the energy you can muster.'

'Me, busy? I told the dogs I'd take them for a stroll down the lane, maybe sit in the field for an hour. Might even take them to the pub later.' She began buttering some toast, a soft smile lighting her beautiful face.

Damn, she fitted right in here. Almost as easily as he did, maybe more so considering those moments he got edgy about trying not to hurt his parents even knowing he would when he left to return to work. His mother always smiled and pretended she was all right with him heading off to places out of the norm to feed his need to fix people, while his dad would shake his hand, say 'Have a good trip' and go out to the shed.

Watching Kristina fork breakfast onto her plate as she chattered with them, Chase knew happiness. *She did fit in here.* And in doing so she was making him feel there was a chance he might, too. 'The dogs really enjoy a good burger and chips washed down with a beer.'

'I thought they might.' She fixed him with a dazzling smile, no trace of her worries of earlier darkening her gaze. 'Verity, what job have you got lined up for me? As long as it's got nothing to do with food, I can do pretty much anything.'

'I was hoping you'd bring the flowers in from the gazebo and arrange them in the lounge.'

She winced. 'I might be better employed dealing with the tables and chairs.'

Chase laughed. 'No flower arranging in the army, then?'

Kristina biffed him on the arm. 'I'll help your dad and you can take care of the flowers.'

His mother laughed, too. 'Whatever. As long as it's all done today. I see Jarrod's pulled up. They'll all want feeding.'

Chase leaned back in his chair and sipped his tea, soaking up the atmosphere. Even when the calm was shattered by three young boys racing into the kitchen shouting 'Happy birthday, Nana' so loudly his eardrums seemed about to burst, he felt the most relaxed he had in…well, in for ever. Funny how his eyes turned to Kristina. Come on. They were always looking her way, seeking her out, watching the play of emotions on her exquisite face, storing images for the months ahead when she was here and he was somewhere else.

Pushing up off his chair, he took his plate, cutlery and mug to the dishwasher. 'Right, let's get this show under way.' He had to get out of here, away from Kristina and her sweet voice as she chatted with *his* family. She was doing his head in, tinkering with his resolve to go solo for ever.

Placing fresh sandwiches and leftover bacon and egg pies on the table hours later, Chase pulled out a chair and sank onto it, trying to ignore the way his body ached in places it had no right to. It showed how out of practice he was when it came to making love. 'Anyone seen Kristina?'

'She took the dogs for a walk,' Libby answered. 'Said she'd be back shortly.'

'One of the dogs has probably taken off after a rabbit. She won't come home without them both in tow.' Tempted to forgo lunch and follow her, he remained seated. Like him, she sometimes needed time alone. He wondered if she was thinking about their lovemaking. It had been out of this world, and a running film kept going across the front of his mind. But with all that came decisions to make. He knew it, and so would Kristina. Nothing had changed in that they still weren't getting together permanently. He had obligations to fulfil—if he ever got around to signing that damned contract. Not once had he taken so long over something as simple as scrawling his name across a piece of paper. Hopefully Kristina wouldn't take so long with Jarrod's offer. She wouldn't be doing herself any favours by procrastinating when it was exactly what she wanted.

His mother was pouring the coffee he'd forgotten. 'Jasper, naughty boy.'

Libby growled, 'No, Jasper, you cannot put all that in your mouth at once. Eat properly.'

Chase's nephew was working at shoving a whole bacon muffin in his mouth. 'Cute.' It was. All part of the family thing, everyone sitting around the table picking at food in a desultory fashion—except for Jasper—mulling over the party and generally relaxing together. He could get used to this all too easily. Where had that dumb idea come from? Usually he was bursting to get out of here before his family dragged him under with their love. But he'd never brought home a woman about whom he cared a lot, hadn't made love in his childhood bedroom since he'd been a horny teenager, and that had been more about sex than love. Face it, he hadn't felt so at ease with the whole scene in a long time.

'It's not cute at all,' Libby growled at him. 'Jasper, behave. You're disgusting.'

The kid couldn't reply with so much food in his mouth.

Chase wanted to laugh because he remembered doing something similar as a boy, but Libby would probably box his ears for encouraging him. Where was Kristina anyway? It was time she came back from her walk and joined in the fun. He'd seen in her demeanour how much she enjoyed interacting with this lot. 'Do you think Kristina will take the position you've offered her, Jarrod?'

'You'd know as much about that as I do,' his brother-in-law answered. 'I know she wants to, but something's holding her back.'

'That'd be Chase, I'm betting.' Libby added her two pence worth.

The hackles rose on the back of his neck. 'Anything Kristina decides has nothing to do with me,' he said a little more forcefully than he'd intended. 'She's quite capable of making up her own mind.'

'Didn't say she wasn't.' Libby grinned. In other words, *Got you, big brother.*

'The job's everything she wants,' he said. 'She likes the town of Merrywood, too. She'll be wanting to buy a house as soon as possible.'

'We're all here for her,' Verity added. 'She can visit any time.'

His family liked getting involved with other people's business, whether asked to or not, but this went further. It was as though they'd accepted Kristina as one of them. He'd witnessed how comfortable she'd been at the medical centre yesterday. The staff had been fighting each other to talk to her. 'Kristina will make up her own mind without anyone putting pressure on her.' She didn't need this lot surrounding her with advice and—

Love?

Yes, from what he knew about them, they probably did love her in their all-embracing way. 'Her independence is important to her. You'd do well to remember that before you try to smother her.'

'Sure you're not talking about yourself, bro?' Libby really had sharpened her tongue overnight.

'That's ridiculous, and you know it,' he snapped. Sometimes Libby went too far. He didn't need to be reminded how he let his family down on a regular basis. 'I'm happy doing the work for *Medicine For All*.'

'Yeah, and when you're done with them you'll find another cause to hide behind. Don't you think it's time to come home and be a part of us again?' Libby gave back as good as she got, more so perhaps.

She had him between a rock and a hard place. Say no and he was telling his family he didn't care about them. Say yes and they'd have interviews at the hospital lined up within days. He went for neutral. 'I'm not ready to stop what I'm doing yet. There are people who need me.' Then the hairs lifted on his skin. Twisting around, he swore under his breath.

Kristina stood in the doorway, sadness darkening her lovely face. Her gaze touched him briefly before she looked away, swallowing hard at the same time. As though she might've been thinking things between them had changed since they'd made love, and had now learned everything was exactly the same.

Guilt had him standing up and pulling out a chair for her. 'Come and have some lunch. Tea?' How much had she heard?

She stepped up beside him and smiled, a slow, soft movement that didn't reach her eyes. Then she turned to his family and said, 'What Chase does for *Medicine For All* is truly amazing and very important. They'd be lost without him.' She sat down and reached for a sandwich.

Libby stared at her, a slow smile finally breaking out and taking the sting out of her next words. 'So, big brother's got to you, too. Don't let that stop you coming to work for us. We need you.'

Kristina chewed and swallowed. 'There's only one person deciding on what I do next and that's me.'

Chase's hands were unsteady as he poured Kristina's tea. She'd had his back in front of his family. He should be squirming. He didn't need anyone taking his side, but while his head railed against that, his heart was lifting, softening. It felt good to have someone who wasn't family caring enough to support him. If he'd thought it was going to be harder than usual to leave the farm today, it was going to be a whole lot harder to say goodbye to Kristina in three weeks' time. Might be best if he backed off before then, stopped seeing her as anything other than a colleague, possibly a friend, but definitely not a woman to make love to in his cabin after he'd finished with the people needing his services.

But first they had the rest of the day to enjoy. Placing the cup in front of Kristina, he said to the room in general, 'How about we go to the pub for a beer before someone drops us at the airport? Let's have some more birthday celebrations. Family only. And Kristina.'

A wicked glint filled his sister's eyes and he wanted to growl at her but refrained. They'd always pressed each other's buttons, and this time he wasn't letting her win. Today was about him and Kristina, before he packed her away and got on with his real life. No, he wasn't exactly proud of himself, but there was no denying the need coursing through his veins.

CHAPTER NINE

'BIG DAY.' THE air was heavy as Kristina leaned on the railing in their corner of the deck. The horizon was lost in grey cloud. Her head was thick due to lack of sleep and a never-ending line of refugees requiring her attention since nine that morning. Many of today's boatload were suffering from fuel burns, and there'd been an outbreak of gastric flu on their cramped boat before they'd been picked up in the Gulf of Sirte.

The sleepless night had been exciting. For most of it. Chase had taken her to his cabin and made love to her with passion and hunger, and a need so great she'd wanted to hold him for ever, reassure him he was safe with her, but she'd held back, uncertain of his reaction. When he'd made love to her a second time he had been so excruciatingly gentle she'd cried. She'd been right to stay quiet. He was saying goodbye to their brief fling. Goodbye to the woman he'd taken to his bed, not to the doctor he'd still be working with.

Around four she'd kissed him softly on his

cheeks and forehead, and lastly on his lips as he'd slept, then she'd crawled out of his bunk to head back to her cabin. He hadn't moved at all.

Now Chase was staring out to sea. 'They happen.' He hadn't budged an inch when she'd joined him. 'It's going to be as hectic throughout the night when the Sudanese refugees arrive.'

The message was so loud, so clear she wanted to shrink in on herself and pretend she was with a complete stranger passing the time of day before going below deck and catching up on much-needed sleep. Throughout the day they'd been so busy the only conversations had been about patients, and those had been abrupt. It was as though once she'd left his cabin that morning she'd left the man she loved, the man who'd let her in close.

Coming up here when it was obvious she wasn't wanted had been a mistake. Was she naïve, thinking he might miss her if she didn't? Damn, but she was pathetic. And hurting, and wishing she could change him, and knowing some things were plain impossible. She'd thought they'd have another three weeks together. Wrong. There weren't going to be any more stolen kisses up here. This area was reverting to *his* space. No making love in his cabin. Nothing.

Well, he wasn't getting away with not talking to her. Kristina watched Chase. 'I got my invitation to Jasper's birthday party today.' She'd checked her emails while downing a hurried meal between patients.

'Me, too.' Still no movement in that lean body she'd touched all over.

'I emailed straight back saying I'd be there.' She'd be living in Merrywood by then. 'His first day of school on the following Monday. How cool's that?'

'They grow up fast.' A sudden yearning flitted through his eyes, then was gone so fast she might've imagined it if she hadn't known what to look for.

Kristina swallowed the hurt she felt for him. She had her own to deal with. He loved his family, and if he thought they didn't know he was fooling himself. He needed shaking—hard. But was it her place to instigate it? No, but when had she ever let something like that stop her? Pressing on, she said, 'You'll be going to the party?'

'I'll be in Africa.' Again that yearning flared, died.

'So you've finally signed the contract?'

He winced and finally looked at her. 'No, but it's lying amongst the paperwork. I'll get to it later tonight.' The bleakness in those eyes was frightening. Did he not understand how much he was hurting himself, let alone everyone else, by being so stubborn about staying on his mission?

'Tell me again why you want to go so far away from those you love?'

'I've told you of my need to help people in difficult or dangerous situations. Nothing's changed, Kristina. There are people all over the world needing urgent medical help that's not easily available. Someone has to be there for them, to save them.' There was a warning in his voice. *Don't step any further over the mark.*

That wound her up fast. 'You think I won't save people in Merrywood? That being a GP in an English town won't rank up there with helping the sick and needy in your foreign locations? That diagnosing a heart condition before it becomes life-threatening isn't saving a life? You think you have to be at the coal face of danger all the time to be a great doctor?' Her disappointment in him, and knowing he wasn't about to change because of anything she said, further cranked up her temper, made it easy to say what she'd held in for days. 'Would you be more accommodating of a relationship between us if I followed you around, doing what you do?'

'No, Kristina, I don't think that. You're brilliant at what you do. I can't imagine you doing anything else. And before you even think it, I am not being condescending. The world needs more of you than of me.' His chest rose slowly. 'Further, I would never expect you to sign up for the work I do—if I even wanted us to be together in a permanent relationship.'

'*Even* if you wanted us to be together?' she choked.

'I don't want to hurt you, but you've never hidden the fact you long to settle in your own home with a career you can become completely involved in. That's what you need, hanker for, have to have, and should make happen. What's more, if you take up Jarrod's offer you're half-way there. Those are the things I don't look for.'

'Avoid, more like.' He hadn't told her anything she didn't already know. But heck. 'Don't turn the conversation onto me,' she snapped around the ache building in her throat. 'You can't handle the heat whenever anyone starts talking about *your* future, can you? Fine, I'll shut up, but don't...' She poked her forefinger into his chest. 'Don't start on what I should be doing.' She'd find a way to accept that she was about to achieve half of what she wanted, which wasn't bad going. Not everyone was so lucky. Unfortunately she'd had a taste of what the other half could be like, and wouldn't be forgetting it in a hurry.

'Fair cop. Talking about my past is the hardest thing I ever have to do, so mostly I don't.' He was in his staring out to sea stance, arms folded across that chest she'd spent so much time kissing, his chin jutting forward with its tempting cover of light stubble, those long, sexy legs tense.

Even in the middle of this she was turned on. Damn him. 'You told me some of what happened in the French mountains.'

His nod was short and sharp. 'I don't regret it. Neither do I regret everything else we've shared,' he added almost as an afterthought, surprise shining out of his eyes for a moment.

Good to know. If it didn't hurt so much. But there was no point carrying on this awkward, snappy conversation. It only undermined the friendship and closeness they had, and if she could keep those alive she would. 'I also emailed Jarrod, accepting his offer.' Somewhere between leaving Chase's cabin and giving her last patient intravenous antibiotics she'd realised the decision was still hers alone to make, and if becoming more involved with Chase's family was the result then she'd grab the opportunity with both hands. He wouldn't stay away because she was there—he already did that.

'It's the right thing to do.' No heart-wrenching Chase smile for her this time. 'If I'm allowed to say so.'

Her heart rolled over. If only it could be different. They understood each other so well they really would work out as a couple—if they weren't looking for completely opposite lives.

'You take care of yourself. I'm sure Libby will keep me up to date with wherever you go and what you do.' To her own ears it sounded like she was saying goodbye. Which she was, despite the weeks ahead on the ship before she left for the final time.

There'd be no resolution for them, no seeing a path they could follow hand in hand. This was not a romance story with the predicable happy ending. Just her luck to fall in love with a man who could not meet her requirements. He was more intent on bashing his head against a brick wall, trying to save every endangered soul on the planet all by himself.

She took a step towards the stairs. It was time to accept what she'd known all along.

'Kristina,' Chase called, and when she turned he was watching her with an intensity that curled her toes and told her heart to move on. 'I am sorry.'

Did he love her at all? A tiny, weeny bit? They'd met equally on more levels than the physical. There'd been gentleness, kindness and, yes, something like love, if not total love, in everything they'd done together, including the times up here. This was the last time she'd come. Why prolong the agony? Stretching up on her toes, she leaned in and kissed him lightly on his mouth. 'I know.'

Then she was gone, out of there, away from the temptation to grovel. She'd only come off worse than she already felt. 'Goodbye, Chase,' she whispered.

Goodbye while they still had to work together. Should be a picnic.

Chase read all the documents that had come in with the medical supplies by boat that morning, signed the ones that were going back in the next outward mail bag, and dropped the rest into the cardboard box that served as his filing cabinet. The clock on the wall read seven-fifteen. Time for dinner, except he wasn't hungry. It had been a week since Kristina had slipped out of his cabin after a night of lovemaking. A week since he'd let her know that whatever they'd had was over. A week of wondering if he'd made the biggest mistake possible, of wishing she'd sneak back into his bed and ignore what he'd said about running alone. A week of growing tired and edgy, of avoiding her, and trying not to let Ethan's presence on board get in the way of his goals and his foul mood.

Pulling a large, over-full envelope towards him, he emptied the contents onto his desk. 'More damned forms to fill in. Why did I train as a surgeon?'

Yeah, why did he? Because of the driving am-

bition to save people's lives, to put them back together when life had made a mess of their bodies,
to make their loved ones happy again. And had
it made him happy?

Ramming his fingers through his hair, he
dropped his head forward and stared at the to-
bacco-coloured carpet between his feet. He didn't
have the right to be happy when Nick had lost
out on so much.

The door opened and the sound of voices and
laughter reached him before the door clicked shut
again. 'Thought I'd find you in here, sulking,'
Ethan said conversationally, before banging a tray
down on the desk.

Chase raised his head and stared at the man
who'd finally become his friend, not his enemy.
'I'm not hungry.' The smell of sausages and chips
made his nose screw up in distaste.

'Sure you're not, but you've got to eat.'

There were two laden plates, two glasses of
iced water and cutlery for both of them. Ethan
had returned for a final stint, as he'd said he
would. He'd been working every hour he could,
and still found time to harass Chase whenever
he thought he needed reminding there was more
to life than this.

'You been talking to Kristina? She told me the
same a while ago.'

'Funny, that. I just gave her the same speech as

I'm giving you. Eat.' Ethan sat down on the other side of the desk and used his fingers to pick up some chips. 'You two had a spat?'

'Not at all.' It was true. They hadn't.

'Then why are you burying yourself in work twenty-four seven? We're busy, sure, but there's more than enough staff to cover everything.'

'I need to catch up on all this.' He waved a hand at the files and documents Ethan had had no compunction about setting the tray on top of. 'I should've been an accountant or statistician, not a surgeon.'

'Getting withdrawal?'

From Kristina? Definitely. 'I sometimes wonder what it might be like working full time as a surgeon in one place, occasionally seeing repeat patients.' His head jerked back and a bleak smile lifted the corner of his mouth. 'Don't know why I'm telling you. You'll find a way to use it against me.' Something Ethan and Kristina had in common—taking what he told them and putting the onus back on him to do something about it.

'Because I know where you're at by rite of the same passage. I'm still getting used to the idea of putting my feet down in one place for as far ahead as I can see. I'll tell you this for nothing. I'm glad I'm doing it. More than glad. Happy beyond anything I could've imagined.'

'I'm happy for you.' Ethan deserved Claire and their unborn child, deserved that happiness.

'So am I.' Ethan chewed on a sausage and watched him. 'It's been quite a roller-coaster ride but I'm glad of every moment so far. I even look forward to the next phase: marriage and parenthood. Who'd have believed I'd be saying that?'

'Not you.'

'Isn't that the truth?' His eyes were still locked on him. Looking for what?

Chase began to feel uneasy, as though Ethan found him lacking. Picking up a handful of fries, he began to eat them one by one, swallowing with difficulty. He'd wait this one out.

Finally, 'You sent that contract back yet?'

It had been lying on the desk for five days, signed and ready to go to head office, gathering dust and more crinkles whenever he fossicked for particular documents to deal with. He shook his head. 'Not yet. But…' he shoved chips into his mouth and picked up the paperwork that would see him fixed up for work over the coming months '… I'll do it right now.'

Ethan's eyes were dark, unreadable as he watched him, more worrying than if he'd been angry.

Chase couldn't help himself. He had to ask. 'What?'

'Why did you ask me to do a spell with MFA?'

Kathump. The sound of his gut hitting the floor was deafening. 'There was that promise you'd come whenever I needed your help. All I had to do was ask.' No cross-examination required. Or wanted.

'What took sixteen years for you to ask? And why ask me for help with something any doctor could do?'

His head joined his gut. 'Could be I wasn't ready to see your face or hear your cheek before.'

'Could be you're starting to think there might be more to life than how you're living? That in order to move on you had to deal with me, with your past—our past—first.'

'Never crossed my mind.' It hadn't. Not once. Never. Why would it?

'I'd been waiting for a damned long time to get that call. Thought it would never come.' A wealth of sadness dulled Ethan's words.

And sapped the resistance out of Chase. 'I wanted to call you, picked up the phone often enough, but then I'd think, Why spoil your day? Then one day I didn't put the phone down, just let the number ring. And here we are. No regrets. Don't ask why that day was any different from the others. It just was.'

'Sure.' Ethan stretched his legs out. 'Make sure you put in the dates you have to be in France for my wedding before you send in that contract.'

He was off the hook, yet relief wasn't rushing at him. 'Plus three days for my nephew's birthday and first day of school.' He owed Libby for upsetting her the morning after their mum's party. Nothing new in that, but he'd decided to go home for Jasper's birthday. If only he'd seen Libby's face when she'd read the email. Probably took an hour to close her mouth.

He had Kristina to thank for this. She'd managed to get him doing things with his family no one else had come close to. Could that be because she'd slotted in so effortlessly? Strange when she wasn't used to a close family who accepted a person for who they were. But if she hadn't had that, it made sense she might grab the opportunity when it came along.

'That's good news.' Ethan shrugged and put his empty plate back on the tray and stole some chips off Chase's. 'What are we expected to reach the next boat of refugees?'

Relief lightened Chase's mood and he stabbed a sausage with a fork. They'd moved past the sticky conversation. 'About six, just in time for breakfast.'

'Then I'll get things set up tonight.'

'You do that and I'll stocktake the pharmaceutical cabinet.' Something else to keep his mind occupied and off Kristina Morton. 'Then Josip wants to go over docking days and when the ship will be laid up for maintenance.'

'I'm sure you can come up with enough to keep you busy until six if you try hard enough.' Ethan sauntered out of the office like he hadn't a care in the world, so unlike the Ethan he'd thought he knew. This new Claire-enhanced version was slowly relaxing into the world around him. Did the man still think back to the avalanche? Of course he did, but he'd learned to go a little easier with what had happened and was beginning to live in the present without having to justify himself and his actions.

All assumption, really, based on how *he* reacted and lived, Chase admitted. He and Ethan had had too little to do with each other over the intervening years for him to be certain about the other man's thoughts and reactions.

Snatching up the drugs list and keys to the cupboard, he headed out of his office.

Less than twenty-four hours to go. Kristina sighed. The weeks since she'd left Chase's bunk had seemed endless and yet now, suddenly, it was all but over, and she'd leave for good in the morning.

The boat was quiet, and time lay heavily on her hands, with no patients needing attention. She'd done a round of those who were left, waiting for tomorrow and disembarkation. She'd accepted thanks and smiles in ever-increasing discomfort. These people deserved to be treated well. No one knew what lay in store for them next.

'Slow night.' Ethan looked up from a book he was reading. 'Claire's looking forward to you visiting for a couple of nights.'

This had felt like the longest period she'd done on the ship, all because Chase took up so much of her mind, and nothing else. The sooner she didn't have to see him countless times, work with him on patients, or hear his voice everywhere she went, the better. 'It'll be great spending time together. Talking baby things and dress shopping for my bridesmaid outfit.' Merrywood Fashion hadn't produced a sky-blue anything, let alone an off-the-shoulder dress fit for the occasion.

Ethan's eye-rolls were quite eloquent when he put in the effort. 'Think I'm washing my hair that day.'

'Thank goodness for small mercies,' she gave back. 'We really don't need your advice.'

'I *am* deciding what I'm wearing to my wedding. Though Claire has given me instructions.' He grinned.

It was amazing how much Ethan had relaxed since meeting Claire. He wouldn't have forgotten anything about the past he shared with Chase but he was so excited about the future it was lovely to see. If only Chase would take the risk, preferably with her. But it wasn't happening, and she had to remember that—all the time.

'Have you got Chase fixed for a suit?' Why ask? Because he was constantly in her mind. It wasn't because she needed to know the groom and his best man had their clothes sorted for the wedding. Claire was more than capable of doing that and, determined woman that she was, she had probably arranged weeks ago everything right down to the socks the men would be wearing.

Ethan's eyebrows rose and he tipped his head ceilingwards. 'What do you think?'

'Yeah, I figured the moment I asked.' Wiping a tissue across her face, she laughed. 'This heat is diabolical. I still haven't got used to it.'

'I know what you mean, and yet we'll be complaining about the cold soon enough.'

'Probably.' That'd be when she was back in England, working as a GP and settling into a routine, maybe even moving into her own little house with lawns and gardens. Like she knew anything about plants and how to look after them. But wasn't that part of putting down roots? Not only her own but those of plants? Learning the day-to-day care and maintenance, pushing the barriers, extending her horizons. Exciting, if she didn't overthink it all. 'I'm heading up on deck for some air.'

Tomorrow she'd step off the ship for the last time. There'd be no coming back. Not that she hadn't enjoyed her time on board. It'd been a great experience, and she'd met lots of wonderful people, including Claire.

Chase. Yes, well. What could she say? She'd found the love of her life, and would be walking away from him. Not that they were together but, still, when the realisation of what little they'd shared was over and got too much to handle she could seek him out, breathe him in, file away more pictures of him working with patients or talking to crew, and pretend she was coping, pretend that her heart would recover, though bruised and wary for a long time to come.

'Your back playing up?' Chase asked from behind as she reached the railing.

Looking around, she gasped softly. She must've been in a different world to have walked into their space without realising he was here. It was the first time since the night she'd said goodbye to Chase and their relationship.

'You're doing the lopsided walk.'

Her hand automatically went to the spot where a steady throbbing had set up in the muscles an hour ago. 'I moved too quickly getting out of the way of some boys chasing a football. I'll have physio when I'm back on land.'

'Not a bad idea.' His smile was friendly, and warmed her down to her toes until he said, 'There was more to the story than being blown up, wasn't there?'

'Why ask now?' Was he tidying up loose ends?

His shoulder lifted. 'I feel I'm missing something.'

'It happened up north in Scotland. No enemy in sight. Something went horrendously wrong and a bomb exploded when there should've been no way it could. Corporal Higgs took a hit in his neck and I was impaled by a steel bar so I had no chance of helping him. I could only focus enough to tell others what to do.' She swallowed. 'Later, I learned nothing would've saved him, but I blamed myself for a long time, even though I understand how it was.'

The bright light from the sun reflecting back at them from the ground, the dust in the air, the silence moments after everything had literally blown up in their faces, the pain, the inability to move—it all raced back to her.

Chase remained where he was, but his arm was now somehow touching hers. 'Leave it if it's too hard.'

She shook her head. 'One day in Merrywood George Baines was electrocuted as I was walking past and I saved him. That made me realise I couldn't win them all and to be grateful for the ones I could. I started getting over the guilt that day.' Something Chase should try and understand.

'We have the guilt in common.'

But not how they dealt with it. 'We do. But neither of us deserves it.'

Chase went back to being silent. What was he thinking? That she'd done what she could and got on with her life in a way he hadn't? Or was he simply wondering why she hadn't settled down in a town as a GP from the moment she'd left the military? Or, even more simply, why was she standing here, talking to him?

'When do you head to Africa?' Might as well jump in and learn all she could to stop those pesky questions zipping around her brain.

'After I've seen Jasper go to school for his first day,' Chase said defensively.

Surprise made her gabble. 'You're going to be there? That's wonderful. Libby will be stoked. So will Verity.'

'Cool it, Kristina. It's no big deal.'

Okay, so he wasn't happy with her. Too late to retract a thing. 'It is to your family.'

'Once you get going, there's no stopping you, is there?' A hint of amusement took the sting out of his words. 'I should be used to it by now.'

'Chase…' How did she put this without sending him running for the stairs?

'Don't, Kristina.'

That automatically stirred her along. 'I was only going to say I'd like it if you'd call in to see me whenever you're visiting your parents. I don't think we need to break contact entirely.' Now she was being pitiful, clutching at any opportunity to see him and thrashing her heart all over again.

'You can count on it.' He gave her a small smile.

'Really?' Down, hope, down.

'Really.'

She'd have to be happy with that.

CHAPTER TEN

THE SHIP ROCKED, causing the gangway to roll as Chase made his way down it for the last time this year. Next stop Ghana.

He paused, waited for the rush of excitement. His heart rate remained the same, his stomach quietly went about its business. Sighing, he continued onto the wharf and stopped, placing his bag at his feet and his hands on his hips as he stared up at the *SOS Poseidon*.

'Will I see you here next summer?' Josip called from the bridge.

'Probably.' Again the exhilaration let him down, not a buzz in his veins at all. 'You take care.'

'I intend to. My wife says she's nailing me to the bed for at least a week.'

Chase laughed. 'Lucky man.' The laughter faded. It wasn't that he was jealous. But not having a woman waiting for him at home, to make love to and talk and laugh with—that made him feel even lonelier than he'd been every damned minute since Kristina had disembarked four weeks ago. No one could ever have made him believe how much he'd miss her. As though she'd taken his heart with her, leaving him struggling to breathe.

The days had crawled by, the nights hadn't moved at all. The hours spent in their space had been cold, despite the soaring temperatures blitzing the region as summer gave one last shove before handing over to autumn. He'd missed Kristina so damned much he ached in every part of his body.

'You going to stand there all day?' Ethan stood near the security gate, hands in his pockets, shaking his head. 'There's a cold one on tap waiting along the road.'

Hoisting his bag, Chase strode across to his friend. 'You're talking sense for once.'

'Who? Me?' Ethan laughed.

Suddenly a lightness settled over Chase. For the next twenty-four hours he could relax, enjoy being with his friend whose best man he'd be as he pledged his love to Claire in a week. 'My shout.'

'Already had that planned.'

They walked along the street until Ethan indicated an English bar. 'I'm missing beer from home.'

With frosty glasses in hand, they settled into a

dark corner. 'Thanks for staying with us,' Ethan said. 'It means a lot.'

Chase took a deep mouthful of beer and swallowed slowly. It felt good, hearing that. 'We've come a long way in a short time.'

'No regrets?'

None whatsoever. 'We should've made the effort years ago.'

'Everything has its time and place.'

'Getting a bit sage, aren't you?' Chase wondered why they'd been at each other's throats so much as teenagers. The need to compete against each other had been huge, but at the expense of friendship? Who understood teenagers?

Ethan stared across the room, the fingers of one hand tapping on the table top, in the other his glass turned round and round. 'How're things with you and Kristina?'

What? 'I'll catch up with her in Merrywood.'

Slowly Ethan brought that inscrutable gaze round to fix on him. 'I don't think I'd have made it with Claire if you and I hadn't begun to repair the past, if we hadn't started to become friends. Without that happening I was too far off the rails, too afraid to trust my instincts when it came to love.'

Where was he going with this? Guys didn't talk amongst themselves about love. There was an awful feeling in the bottom of Chase's gut suggesting he wasn't going to like whatever came out of the man's mouth next, and he rushed in to halt him. 'You're moving on. That's enough.'

'You're in love with her.'

Chase sucked in stale air, stared at the apparition he'd thought he was getting to know. 'You think?'

'What are you going to do about it?'

'Nothing.' Was that admitting he did love Kristina? As in with all his heart loved her? 'I'm heading to Ghana straight after your marriage ceremony. Do you seriously think I should persuade Kristina to join me when she's finally found the life she wants?'

'What's wrong with you stopping in one place long term with her?'

'You know why I can't do that. More than anyone, you understand.'

'Before Claire I'd have agreed with you. Even after Claire I might've for a while. Not now.'

'Okay, you've found what you were looking for but—'

'I wasn't looking to settle down, certainly didn't intend to get married and become a dad for the same reasons you're denying yourself love. I was always looking for places to be, towns to slip through on the way to the next hellhole where people needed my undivided attention to make them better.' He banged his empty glass on the table. 'I was you. You are who I used to be.'

Chase sat back, gobsmacked. There was nothing to say. He didn't understand, didn't *want* to understand the message Ethan was banging him over the head with. He could admit to himself he loved Kristina. To tell her would only hurt, because he'd have to follow up with the statement that he didn't intend to do anything about it. She already knew that. 'Want another?' He nodded at the empty glasses between them. If only that was all that lay between them, but it seemed Ethan was hell bent on prodding old wounds.

'Sure.'

Moving through the throng of men standing at high tables eating lunch with their beers, Chase fought the urge to run for the exit. What right did Ethan have to talk about his love for Kristina? He'd never admitted his feelings out loud, afraid that by voicing them he wouldn't be able to keep them under wraps. That was where they had to stay. For Kristina's sake. If that wasn't love, what was?

Back at the table they sat in silence as the beer slowly disappeared down their throats. Chase began to relax. That conversation was done. Now he could enjoy a night with his friend and Claire. It was such an alien idea that it excited him. 'How long does it take to drive to Claire's apartment?'

Ethan downed another mouthful of his beer, drew a breath, and locked his eyes on the table between them. 'Stop trying to save everyone, Chase. It's not possible. I know. We're sorry examples of men when it comes to what we want from life, but Claire has shown me otherwise. You…' his finger tapped the table top '…can have what you're hankering after—Kristina and love and a family, all in your own corner of the world. You want that as much as you want to save those people, so go about it differently. Get a job back home. I'm learning that saving a child by removing a ruptured appendix in a big hospital is as rewarding as debriding a refugee's burns. You can have it all. Go for it, man. You're entitled to happiness. We both are.'

There wasn't anything to say. It would take time to absorb the sincerity in Ethan's words, and even then Chase doubted if he could accept the possibility of following suit. 'You're staying on in France, not moving back to England?'

'Claire needs to be where she is, and that's enough for me. Have to admit I'm not keen on spending too much time with her family with the mountains that loom over their village, but as long as I don't go climbing or skiing I'll manage.' He drained his glass. 'And I need you here next week. I'm not waiting any longer to get married.'

There he went again. It all came back to the

love of a good woman. Apparently Ethan would do anything to make his woman happy. Anything.

Wasn't that what he was doing by staying out of Kristina's way? Making her happy rather than dragging her around the world as he saw fit?

Ethan picked up their empty glasses. 'Let's hit the road. Gridlock starts when everyone heads out of the city at the end of work, and Marseille in gridlock is hell on wheels.'

Conversation was on hold until Ethan pinged the locks of his SUV. 'One last thing, then I'll shut up. We can't undo the past but we can change our futures. Start doing something about that now. Not tomorrow, not next month, now. Go home, stop wandering the globe.'

Chase's pack dropped into the back of the SUV with a loud thud. 'Never knew you could talk so damned much,' Chase snapped around the pain that was flaring in his belly and spreading throughout his body. Did Ethan believe he could change his life with the snap of his fingers? When he knew better than anyone what held him back?

But he does know. That's the whole point.

Was it possible to turn his life around?

Did he want to?

He was beginning to think he did.

And he knew where he had to start.

* * *

The hut sat on the brow of the hill behind the copse, the door closed but not bolted. The front was bathed in weak sunlight. The weatherboards had recently been painted. Dad doing his regular upkeep even when this particular tiny building had not been used since Nick had died.

Chase sat on the edge of the veranda and leaned back against the wall, deliberately letting the ache come and the memories start opening. Gazing out over the green pastures, he wished he'd brought a bottle of beer to raise to Nick. 'We were going to conquer the world, live in the fast lane, you as an architect and me a plastic surgeon. Women were going to fall at our feet, we were going to make millions, own our own houses and take holidays in exotic locations.'

Despite the tears tracking down his cheeks, he laughed. 'We were morons. Normal teenagers from secure backgrounds who knew the only way to get ahead was by working hard, and then harder still, and yet we dreamed.'

What a lot of fun they'd had up here, drinking illicit beers and talking nonsense. At least they hadn't been on the street, doing drugs or getting drunk, robbing the local grocer.

The biggest and likeliest dream had been that the team would win the European under-eighteens ski championships. 'You would've made it, mate. It was a given. You deserved to win.'

He sat looking down on the world that had been his childhood, his safe place, his home, and thought about Nick, then the night that everything had changed for ever, Ethan, and lastly Kristina. 'I love her, Nick. Everything about her. She's gutsy and strong and sweet and sexy, and why am I telling you this?'

Focusing on the farm, a sense of belonging stole through him. This *was* his place. He'd never live in the house again. His children wouldn't grow up with these paddocks to run around in, and this hut would not be their hideaway, but his heart belonged here.

It also belonged to Kristina. If she'd accept him as he was—flawed, wounded, and willing to give life a go with no guarantees.

The sun was dropping beyond the distant hedges when Chase finally roused himself. Time to get started on the future. But first he had to close the past. He stood, hands in his pockets, feet splayed, and his eyes closed. 'Nick, I'm sorry, buddy, but the time has come for me to let you go. It's not fair you didn't get to do any of those things you wanted so much, and I've done everything I can to make up for that in other ways. Now I'm done.' He opened his eyes, looked around and felt okay about what he was doing. 'Goodbye, Nick.'

That night Chase slept the deepest sleep he could remember having. In the morning he joined his parents for breakfast then borrowed his father's four-wheel drive and headed into the city.

'Thank you so much, Dr Morton. Sorry to be a nuisance but I panicked when Lily went limp and quiet.' Sherry bounced a now happy baby in her arms.

'Stop apologising. I'd rather you came in and there was nothing wrong than you stay away because you're embarrassed and we find there's something to worry about. Most first-time mothers are the same.' Kristina tickled Lily on the chin. 'Your mother loves you, gorgeous.'

Sherry nodded. 'I still can't believe how that just happens, no warning, nothing. One day I was pregnant, and the next I was holding this precious little bundle I'd give my life for if I had to.'

Kristina's heart squeezed. Would she ever know the same love? 'Let's hope it never comes to that.' Placing Lily's file on the receptionist's counter, she picked up her next patient's notes. 'I'll see you for Lily's six-month check-up. Unless you're worried about anything before then.'

Sherry nodded. 'I'm so glad you're back.'

Sherry's words registered in the back of her

mind as she scanned the waiting room for Mrs Winter and instead found Chase sitting, watching her. Every thought went out of her mind as her blood heated and her body turned in his direction. He was sexier even than her memory of him, and that was off the scale. Those magical hands lying loosely on his thighs dried her mouth as more memories flooded her head. 'I've missed you so much.'

'I've missed you, too.' Chase crossed to her, those hands reaching for her, taking her close to that wicked chest.

She hadn't seen him move, didn't know she'd spoken aloud until his reply. He'd missed her? Really? In the way she hoped? 'I didn't know you were in town.' Libby hadn't mentioned it. Though Claire and Ethan were getting married shortly, so she should've figured he'd turn up.

'I got in yesterday.' His hands dropped away. His hug had been brief but warm. Friendly.

Ah, friendly. He hadn't come specifically to see her. But he'd said he'd missed her. What was going on? 'You're waiting to see Jarrod?' Not her. They weren't an item. She was getting on with her life, not stagnating while waiting for Chase to make random appearances.

'No.' His hand reached for hers again. His tongue licked his bottom lip. 'I—I'm hoping you'll spare me some time after you finish up. Go for a meal at the pub?'

'Oh.' She gulped. 'Oh.' Where was the strong, know-what-I-want Chase? This nervous version was new to her. 'I'd like that.'

There was relief going on in that gaze locked on her. 'I'm early, but I didn't want to risk you leaving before I saw you.'

'I've got two more patients.' Kristina dragged her eyes away to look around the room for her next patient, trying to get her brain functioning properly.

'I'll be here.'

She began to turn away.

'Kristina?' She turned back, still trying to fathom what was going on. "I'm glad you missed me,' he said quietly.

Thud. Was that her heart hitting the floor? 'Meaning?' She needed to find another doctor quickly because she was in no state to take care of patients. Not after that. Chase was either building her hopes up or about to kick her feet out from under her.

'Talk to you later.' His hand cupped her chin for a moment, dropped away. 'I'm not here to hurt you, okay?'

Okay? Her head dipped into a nod without thought. 'Fine.' Whatever that meant. First she had to get a grip. Just because Chase had strolled into her day didn't mean forgetting what, who her day was meant to be about. 'Mrs Winter?'

An elderly woman rose stiffly, and hobbled her way. 'Hello, dear. Are you Dr Morton, then?'

'I am. Pleased to meet you.' With all her will-power Kristina remained focused on the lovely lady before her and ignored the man who'd once again thrown her mind into a flap. 'Come through, and tell me what's bothering you today.'

Removing what appeared to be a basal cell carcinoma from Mrs Winter's lower arm took half an hour and made Kristina late for her last patient, who didn't seem fazed.

'I've been talking to Chase Barrington,' Tony Webster told her as he sat down by her desk. 'We went to school together. He always was a great guy. If only he'd come home.'

See what you're missing out on, Chase? People who know you and want to be a part of your life are as important as the ones you see briefly before they disappear over the horizon on their own journeys.

'He's doing a wonderful job with *Medicine For All*.' Why had he asked her out for a meal? 'What can I do for you today, Tony?'

'It's my hip, Doc. It's getting more painful and I need to increase the diclofenac.'

The joint had been fractured a year ago when a cow had charged him, and he'd had problems

ever since. 'It might be time for that hip replacement.' The wait-and-see approach hadn't worked
and Tony needed to face facts. 'Up on the bed
and I'll have a look.' After getting him to lift his
leg, push sideways as she assessed his resistance
level, Kristina returned to her desk and brought
up the radiology request form. 'Get dressed. I'm
sending you for an X-ray and referring you to the
orthopaedic department.' She typed in details,
printed off a radiology form and a repeat pre-
scription for his anti-inflammatory drug.

'Only old people have hip replacements.'

Men. Stubborn creatures. Why *was* Chase
waiting for her to finish work? 'Let's see what
the X-ray shows, shall we?'

'I can't afford to take time off from the farm.'

'You'd rather lie awake in pain every night and
hobble around the fields at half your speed. I
get it. Make that appointment with Radiology
today.' Then she glanced at her watch. 'Tomorrow. I'll be following up on you.' She smiled to
soften the blow.

'I'm docking sheep tomorrow.' He limped out,
a scowl on his face.

'Nice try,' Kristina called after him, before
closing down the computer. Picking up her bag
and keys, she slung her denim jacket over one
shoulder and went to find Chase. And learn what
this was about.

Pausing at the door, her gaze filled with the sight of him leaning against the reception counter, talking with Jarrod. Even knowing Chase was here hadn't prepared her for the simple need to throw herself at him and wrap her arms around that tall, lean body, to feel his muscles under her palms and breathe in his man scent, just… Oh, just whatever. She'd missed him beyond reason. Missed the intimacy, his sexiness, their talks, everything about the guy. *Settle down, girl.* One evening sharing a meal wouldn't change a thing. He'd still head away on another adventure come tomorrow.

When he took her elbow, sparks flew up her arm. 'You all right to walk?' he asked calmly. No sparks for him?

'Definitely. I need to get the kinks out of my back. There's a lot of sitting with this job.' Which was never good.

'You been going to physio?'

'Twice a week. There's a physiotherapist connected to the medical centre, which is handy.' And the woman knew what she was doing. Always a bonus.

Chase placed two beers on the table and sat opposite Kristina so he could watch her face. He'd missed how her expression lightened when she laughed, how her eyes went deep blue in serious moments, how she scratched whatever surface was available with her forefinger when discussing those things that had shaped her life.

The moment he'd seen her in the waiting room he'd wanted to scoop her up and run to the nearest hotel room to make love, to show her how special she was. 'Jarrod tells me you've settled into the medical centre without any hitches.'

'It's early days yet.' She blushed.

He hadn't seen that before, and tenderness stirred throughout him. 'You've made the right move.'

The light blue shade of her eyes turned dark as she gave a sharp nod. 'It's working out well. I'm going to look at two houses next week that have just come on the market. In for the job, in for everything.'

'You don't think you're rushing things?' She could come a cropper if she suddenly wanted to up stakes and head off somewhere else. Houses didn't always sell overnight.

'If I don't back myself, how can I expect anyone else to?'

She had an answer for everything. Way ahead of him. But he was racing to catch up. 'Point taken.'

'Hey, Kristina, see you at the make-up party on Saturday?' A woman in her thirties stood by their table.

'You sure will, Pam.'

See? She was fitting in in a way he struggled to envisage, yet was finally willing to give a shot. He'd listened to the young mother with her baby talking to the receptionist about how kind and caring Dr Morton had been, and how she was glad to have her as her doctor, and felt he was missing out on something big. When Tony came out of her room looking like he'd lost a battle, and grumping about Doc thinking she knew best, Chase had known exactly how he felt.

Weeks back when Kristina had had a crack at him about how he could do as much good for people here as anywhere he'd gone all defensive, believing she didn't understand what drove him. He wasn't going to be sucked into her way of thinking that home was best, didn't want to get involved with her or the town he'd run away from. Then Ethan had added his two euros' worth, saying the same thing even more directly. Who knew better than Ethan where he was coming from?

Throw in the four longest, dullest, most boring weeks of his life out at sea, and he knew he had to stop holding out for the lonely path he'd chosen when he'd been at his lowest. He had to do something different or end up a bitter, lonely old man with only himself to blame.

Kristina. He loved her. Without reservation.

Would the woman hurry up and leave? He had things bugging the hell out of him to share with Kristina. Now. Not later.

'Thanks for the invitation.' Kristina lifted her glass and took a sip.

The woman got the hint and said goodbye.

'You're popular already.' He needed to provoke that sweet blush, and was instantly rewarded.

'Join the medical centre, join the whole town.' Her smile was strained.

'That's how it is here, people watching out for each other.'

Her eyebrows rose, but she kept quiet.

'Everyone turned out to support me after the avalanche. I was overwhelmed by their compassion.' And his grief, but he'd put that to bed yesterday. 'I've spent the day visiting hospitals and surgical practices in Taunton and Frome. I'm looking for a job.'

Kristina leaned back in her chair, her eyes locked on him, disbelief warring with hope in her expression. 'Say that again.'

'I'm coming home, Kristina. It's time.'

'Why?'

'Because if I don't do it now, the chances are I never will, and I need to as much as I needed to stay away before.' Everything was so clear—how he'd wasted his life rushing after causes, how he'd let his family down when all they'd ever done was love and support him. But more than that, 'It's you. I love you. I want that future you're following. I want to...' He ran out of words as he watched Kristina's reaction.

Never a big talker, she was now silent. Shocked might best describe her. Her eyes remained locked on him, her hands tight around her glass.

'Say something,' he croaked.

She picked up her drink in unsteady hands and gulped a mouthful, all the while watching him.

Raucous laughter broke out on the other side of the room.

Chase stood up and took the glass out of Kristina's hands, placed it on the table, then took her hand and tugged gently. 'Let's get out of here.' What had he been thinking to drop that on her when surrounded by people that had nothing to do with this conversation?

Outside he led her to the four-wheel drive he'd borrowed from his father that morning, and held the passenger door open as she climbed in. 'Where're you living?'

'Are you sure?'

'That I love you? Yes.'

'It's a bit sudden, isn't it?' Her tongue worried the corner of her mouth.

'I believe it started the day we worked together to save Antoine on the wharf. I didn't recognise love for what it was, or, if I did, I didn't want to.'

She had to believe him. He wasn't making any of this up.

Kristina turned her startled gaze forward, so he couldn't read her any more. Not that he was having much luck interpreting what she was thinking anyway. 'Take me to the river. I need to walk.'

It would be dark soon, but the idea of being shut inside the house with Chase while she absorbed what he'd told her made Kristina feel hot and cold all at once. She needed space, not walls closing in on her.

Chase loves me. Who said dreams didn't come true? Her wildest dream had been that he'd fall for her and want to settle down here. So why wasn't she falling into his arms with excitement? Did she love Chase? Without a doubt.

Chase loves me.

So he'd been looking for work in the area. How long would he stay in one job before that crippling need to be actively helping those unfortunate people took over? Would he be able to stop in one town long term?

You have. It was early days, but she already knew she'd found her corner of the world. She was happy here—when she wasn't thinking about Chase. Sure, there'd be times when things went wrong, but this was home. But could Chase do the same?

He was pulling over. 'This do?'

'Yes.' The river walkway was devoid of locals, thank goodness. Now was not the time to be making idle chitchat. She slid out of the vehicle and pulled on her jacket, zipped it up against the cool evening air. 'How did the job hunt go?' she asked as they began strolling along the river's edge.

'I have an interview tomorrow with the head of surgery at Collingwood Hospital. There are no positions right now, but there might be one coming up. In the meantime, I'll keep door knocking. Jarrod's contacting two surgeons in private practice he knows well.'

'You sound...excited.'

Chase looked down at her. 'You know what? I am. Now I've made up my mind I'm keen to get cracking on starting over.' Then his smile faded. 'You're not certain I'll stay around, are you? You're worried that I'll wake up one morning and wonder whatever possessed me to give up the life I've led for so long.'

'Yes, that's exactly what's going through my mind.' *I'm terrified my heart will be broken.* At the moment she could walk away and it would only be badly bruised, but to believe they had a future and then have it torn away—no, she couldn't survive that. 'I'm sorry.'

'It's right that you're looking out for yourself. I understand that.' Wrapping an arm over her shoulders, he pulled her out of the way of a cyclist. 'I'm going to Ghana the day after Ethan and Claire tie the knot.'

Her heart slowed. See? He hadn't made the change yet, was still hanging onto the old life. 'You finally signed the contract.'

His body touched the length of hers, strong and warm, making her want to believe in him. 'Yes, in a fit of uncertainty I did. I was grappling with missing you so damned much it hurt. Do I regret it? No, because I owe Liam time to find my replacement. Anyway, the contract is only for four weeks.'

Not long enough to know he'd made the right decision. Or was it? Was she being fair? Just because it had taken her a couple of years to realise the army couldn't give her what she'd been looking for, it didn't mean Chase needed as long. Kristina began walking again, pleased when Chase's arm remained around her shoulders. She'd missed him so much there'd been days when she'd wondered if she should walk away from what she'd found and re-join him on the ship. 'Four weeks and then you're moving to Somerset.'

'For good, Kristina. For good. This is where my heart is.'

She stopped in the fading light and turned into him, looking up at that face that was seared into her mind. 'I'm glad. You belong here. I've wanted to bang you over the head so you'd see what you've been missing out on.'

'Trust me, you did that more than once.' His smile was wry. 'Verbally, and in the way you fitted in with people I care about. That woke me up more than anything. If you could let your past go and be happy in a town that was new to you, slotting in as though you'd always lived here, why couldn't I return to where I'd grown up and have known people my whole life?'

'Because you're stubborn?' She raised an eyebrow and grinned, letting the wonder of his love take hold.

'There's that.' He grinned back. Then sobered. 'Kristina, I meant what I said. I love you with all my heart.'

She'd never told him how she felt. True, she had doubts about his ability to stay put, but while she'd only known his restless side she'd seen his strength in dealing with the day-to-day dramas and tragedies on the *Poseidon*. And he loved her.

'I want to marry you and settle into a home of our own and eventually fill the spare bedrooms with kids that have fair hair and summer-blue eyes,' he added.

Tears streaked down her face. 'Really?' she choked. Wasn't this what she'd been searching for?

'What do you think?' he asked as his arms wound around her.

Drawing herself up and taking a deep breath, she told him, 'You need to know I love you, too.' She'd always wanted the chance to love someone and to be loved back. And here it was. *Chase*. 'Yes, Chase, I love you,' she repeated.

'Oh, sweetheart.' His mouth touched hers, soft and warm and filled with love. The kiss when it came was long and slow and made her heart melt.

She didn't think it could get any better.

Chase lifted his mouth away from hers. 'Kristina, please say you'll marry me.'

Seemed she still got things wrong. This went beyond better. 'As soon as you return home for good.'

'Better start planning the wedding. From what Ethan tells me, it's quite a process.'

'Claire doesn't have Verity or Libby alongside her.'

'True.' Chase smiled. 'Family. They're going to be thrilled about this.'

'Want to go tell them now?'

He shook his head. 'No. We're going back to your place and I'm going to make love to you all night long.'

'Perfect answer, husband-to-be. Perfect answer.'

EPILOGUE

'I DECLARE YOU man and wife,' the marriage celebrant announced with a smile. 'You can now kiss your— Oh, right… Well, it seems I was a bit slow off the mark.'

Kristina would've laughed but she was too busy returning Chase's enthusiastic kiss. They'd done it. Gone and got themselves hitched, surrounded by family and friends.

'Okay, you two. There are children present.' Ethan clapped Chase on the back. 'Plenty of time for that later.'

Chase dragged his mouth away. 'Go and annoy *your* wife, will you?'

'Oh, no, you don't,' Claire shot back as Ethan reached for her.

Kristina grinned as she slipped her arm through Chase's. 'Get in line, you guys.'

'Did I tell you she's ex-military?' Chase turned back to Ethan.

'Didn't need to. I've known who's in charge in this relationship right from the start.'

'You haven't seen anything yet.' Taking her first step in her now complete life, Kristina tugged her husband and began the walk down between the chairs where everyone important to them stood and cheered.

Even her father, who reached out and placed a gentle dad kiss on her cheek. 'You're beautiful, my girl.'

On the other side of the aisle her mother dabbed at her eyes and nodded. For once her mum appeared to be in tune with her father.

Tears spilled down Kristina's carefully made-up face and she couldn't have cared less. The photos would show the real emotions of the day, smudged mascara and all. Her family mightn't know how to express aloud their love for her, but today they'd shown it by being here. It was all she asked.

Outside the tiny village church in the wintry sunshine they crossed the road to the wedding reception venue and were met by a waiter holding a tray of glasses filled with champagne and one with sparkling water for Claire. The four of them formed a tight circle and clinked the glasses. 'To the four of us,' Chase said.

'To us,' Ethan agreed.

After taking a sip, Chase dropped a kiss on Kristina's cheek then locked his gaze with Ethan's. 'We did it. Both of us.'

Ethan's hand splayed across against Chase's back. 'No regrets. This is real, and wonderful, and, yes, we made it.'

Chase looked at Ethan, then her. And raised his glass as he looked upward. 'To Nick.'

'To Nick.' Ethan nodded.

Kristina's tears grew heavier, but her heart was light. 'They're special, our men,' she whispered to Claire.

'I'm so glad they're happy, and have found a way forward.'

'I'll drink to that,' Kristina agreed.

'So will we,' Chase added as he smudged a streak of mascara off her cheek.

'Big ears.' His wife grinned. Tears maybe, but nothing today was going to wipe the smile off her face.

Then Libby was nudging into the group, breaking the moment, only to replace it with another. 'Welcome to the family, Kristina.' Then she broke down. 'And thank you for making Chase see sense at last.'

'Another glass required over here.' Chase beckoned a waiter.

Then they were surrounded by people congratulating them.

'It doesn't get any better than this, does it?' Chase whispered in Kristina's ear.

'Well...' She tapped her mouth thoughtfully.

'Don't.' He laughed. 'I love you. That's all you're getting.'

'That's all I need.'

* * * * *

If you missed the previous story in the
SOS Docs duet, look out for

Saved by Their One-Night Baby
by Louisa George

And if you enjoyed this story, check out
these other great reads from
Sue MacKay

The Italian Surgeon's Secret Baby
ER Doc's Forever Gift
Surprise Twins for the Surgeon
Baby Miracle in the ER

All available now!